The blade of betrayal cuts deep…

When Erica is granted a commission in the king's army and gifted a magical sword for her bravery, she begins to look forward to a future for both herself and her crew. But not everyone is happy with their circumstances.

Erica joins Brenn's team in the fight to save his planet from the angry god, Zohmes, and she finds herself charmed by more than just the planet. The sexy lion shifter, Laro, claims she is his lifemate, setting her passions ablaze. Stung by the sharp tongues and dissension of some of her crew, Erica pushes him away to focus on the lives of her crew members.

Can Erica accept a future with Laro, or will she let hate and betrayal decide her fate?

Sword of Betrayal
Crimson Realm Chronicles Book 3
Copyright © 2018 Taryn Jameson and Gabriella Bradley
ISBN: 978-1-4874-1761-1
Cover art by Angela Waters

Published by eXtasy Books Inc

Look for us online at:
www.eXtasybooks.com or www.devinedestinies.com

SWORD OF BETRAYAL

CRIMSON REALM CHRONICLES
BOOK 3

BY

TARYN JAMESON AND GABRIELLA BRADLEY

DEDICATION

Taryn Jameson: To my husband, who always makes sure to leave me at least half the pot of coffee, even if it is several hours before I get my first cup.

Gabriella Bradley: To my family, friends, and our faithful readers...

CHAPTER ONE

Erica pivoted in front of the mirror, her long, emerald-green gown edged with gold embroidery swinging around her legs. Matching green sandals encased her feet. "I still think I should wear my captain's uniform."

"Captain, you know what Brenn told us. We need to dress according to their customs," Laura said while making adjustments to her shoulder-length blonde hair.

"At home, for such an important event, we would be required to appear in full uniform."

"Except we're not on Earth. We need to adapt to their ways. This is not going to be an ordinary wedding by any means. We should feel honored that they invited the whole crew," Lisa, their biologist, said.

Erica nodded. "True. Only some are invited to witness the ceremony in the Clyss, close family, the king, and closest friends. It's just that I don't feel comfortable wearing a dress. I grew up wearing jeans, then bodysuits once we entered the space program. Never dresses." *Except for one,* but she pushed the memory of her wedding gown out of her mind.

"Erica, you look beautiful. Except for that short hair of course. Your hair is such a gorgeous red, and those curls. I don't know why you ever cut it." Catrice finger-combed through her own honey brown hair.

Erica grimaced and glanced at her reflection, tucking a stray curl behind her ear. "I think I had a moment of rebellion against getting stranded on an alien planet in a different universe. It'll grow again."

"Are you sorry we're stranded here? We've all been wondering. You've been so busy gallivanting around on exciting missions with hot men and staying at the house of one of them. We haven't seen you for a while. I'm glad you at least decided to join us to prepare for this event," Jill, one of their nurses, said.

"Honestly? I had mixed feelings at first, but now that we've been here for a while, I'm beginning to accept that we're going to live out our lives on Ierilia. I do worry about the other ships, though, wondering if they made it to their destination. I can't help thinking about them."

"We'll never know, will we? I'm surprised you've found time to think about them at all as busy as you were. And of course, you're smitten over that guy we met at the engagement party. What's his name again?" Jill asked.

"Laro, and he's hot," Catrice said.

Erica frowned. "I am *not* smitten. He's just a sweet guy and has become a friend. I spent a lot of time with him and the others when we went to rescue Icaras and on our other missions."

"It would have been nice if we could have gone along on some of those missions instead of being back in school, learning their language and doing boring research about Ierilia's history," Jill complained.

Erica looked Jill in the eyes. "I'm sorry some of you are unhappy at the state of events. But it is what it is. We have to make the best of it and learn to adapt. But come. We need to join the men and meet Aldis."

The men were already waiting. Erica glanced at them and noticed John Watering was decked out in his full officer's uniform. "John, go to your room and please change into the clothes provided."

"I don't feel like playing medieval dress-up," he said in a tone of rebellion.

"Do as you're told, John. And hurry up. Aldis is waiting for us. Otherwise, stay here," Erica commanded.

For a moment, she thought he'd defy her, but then he swiveled angrily and stalked back to the men's rooms. "We'll wait for him."

He didn't take long, as asked, and appeared in the finery provided for him. Erica nodded her approval. "Let's go."

They headed to the landing pad, where two flyers waited. Aldis stood beside one, looking very distinguished in his uniform. He wore his dark auburn hair shorter than the other men, just long enough to pull in a queue at the nape of his neck. If she had to guess his age, he appeared to be in his forties. His hair was lightly laced with gray at the temples and laugh lines framed his striking amber eyes. He walked toward Erica, his hands held out. "You look lovely, Erica. You'll fly with me and my mate, along with ten of your crew. The other flyer will transport the others."

"Thanks for the compliment, Aldis. I'm excited and feel honored that we all received an invitation."

"The king felt it important that you and your crew become completely familiar with all our customs and traditions," Aldis said as he waited for the Earth crew to enter the flyer and take their seats.

Aldis and Erica entered last, Erica taking the seat behind Aldis. "Erica, this is Janarta, my mate."

Erica smiled at the woman seated next to Aldis. "It is lovely to meet you, Janarta. You have a very brave husband."

"Husband?" Janarta queried.

"Sorry. Earth language for mate. Aldis, where are your children?"

"They will be present at the festivities at Brenn's estate following the ceremony. Except for being presented to the gods and goddesses at birth, children are not allowed in the Clyss."

It took hardly any time for them to arrive at the Clyss. Aldis landed the craft on a grassy field. As Erica stepped out of the flyer and onto the steps, she gasped at the beauty she faced. "Oh, my God. This is paradise!"

Standing on the grass, surrounded by her crew, she gazed at the scenery. Everywhere she looked were trees bearing an abundance of red-and-white flowers. The shrubs beneath them were also in full bloom in every color of the rainbow. A distance away a waterfall fed a pristine pool of water. Close to the pool, a small gathering sat on the grass.

"Follow me," Aldis said while taking his mate's hand and walking toward the guests on the grass.

Erica scanned the people. "I don't see Brenn and Ciara anywhere."

"Now that we are all here, they will arrive shortly," Aldis told her. He instructed her crew to sit on the grass but motioned Erica to follow him.

Erica was surprised she had to sit at the front. "Who performs the ceremony?"

"In this case, King Biryn will unite the couple, and the goddess Rania will bless the union."

"She will appear?"

"Yes. This union is very special, one like Ierilia has never experienced. The gathering is small. There was no time to send out official invitations to all heads of the various realms."

A hush fell over the people as several dragons appeared above them. They descended and landed near the flyers. Their transformation was almost instant. Erica gasped as Ciara's parents walked toward them. They looked magnificent in their royal finery. They stood beside the lake on the silvery sand.

Another dragon appeared, her mauve-and-purple scales shimmering in the suns' rays. Brenn sat atop her. As he slid down and stood to wait for his bride to change to her human, Erica noticed he wore his full warrior gear. Ciara, now as her human, held out her hand. He took it, and they walked toward her parents. She looked breathtaking in her scintillating white dress. A purple silk robe embroidered with small silver moons at the edges draped from both shoulders, held there by jeweled clasps. Her waist-long black wavy hair cascaded naturally down her back, adorned by a glittering silver tiara set with precious stones.

"She's absolutely gorgeous and looks so happy," Erica whispered.

King Biryn stood up, not far from where Erica sat. Though she'd seen the king quite a few times now, his mode of dress had always been quite simple. He was dressed in full royal regalia. A gold crown, embedded with red jewels that matched his red, gold-embroidered tunic, rested on his head. His long brown hair shimmered with golden highlights in the sun. He wore black tights with black leather boots up to his knees. At his side she noticed a beautiful golden sword, almost the same as Brenn's. A red cape, edged with gold braid and lined with gold silk, draped from his shoulders.

Biryn joined the couple beside the pool. Brenn and Ciara had joined hands. He faced them, then raised his arms and held up his hands, palms upward, and looked up at the sky. "May the gods and goddesses smile upon you both this day. As ruler of Ierilia, I will now unite you both, one to the other."

King Brokig and Queen Iede stepped toward them. Biryn lowered his arms and turned to them. "Brokig and Iede, rulers of the Tideless Abyss, do you give permission for your daughter to join with Brenn Mildash? Do you welcome him as a son?"

"We do," they said in unison.

"Princess Ciara of the Tideless Abyss, do you wish to leave the home of your parents and be joined to this warrior of King Biryn's army?"

"I do."

"General Brenn Mildash, do you wish to take Princess Ciara as your eternal mate?"

"I do."

A woman brought a garland of white flowers to the king. He draped it around the couple's necks as if binding them together. "Love is as fragile as these flowers. Guard it well. Treasure it. Be true to it. Honor one another. By my authority as king of Ierilia, you are now mated for all eternity. May the gods and goddesses bless you richly. And now, you will undergo the purification ceremony as is traditional in our realm."

Ciara undid the clasps of her robe and let it drop to the sand. To Erica's amazement, Brenn began to divest himself of his general's uniform until he stood wearing nothing but a loincloth. Ciara dropped her gown and stood naked before them, only a gauzy bit of cloth held by a gold chain around her hips hung in gentle folds to her knees, barely covering her pubic area.

Several women approached, carrying small containers. They carefully removed the floral garland. "What are they doing?" Erica asked softly.

"Just watch. Don't speak," Aldis whispered.

The women worked swiftly. To Erica's consternation, using their fingers, they began to paint Ciara and Brenn, starting with their faces. Brenn's design was mostly of suns, yellows and oranges almost depicting sunsets on some of the larger areas of his body. On Ciara, they painted the moons and small stars.

6

Erica was amazed how fast they worked and how accurate they were. She couldn't help but feel turned on by the virtually erotic scene, though there was no sexual activity. It was just so sensual the way the women painted Ciara's and Brenn's bodies and how they moved around the couple in fluid movements appearing as if they were dancing. After the women finished painting the couple's arms, Ciara and Brenn lifted them above their heads. They parted their legs, and their buttocks received the same treatment. Except for their pubic area, there was practically no skin visible. Last, the women painted their feet, then hastened away, leaving Brenn and Ciara each with a small jar. Ciara unclasped the gold chain, and the piece of cloth fell to the grass. Brenn did the same with his loincloth. Erica drew in her breath. Without thought, she placed her hand on Laro's leg and squeezed. She had no idea what to expect next. Surely they wouldn't mate in front of everyone?

Brenn stepped toward Ciara. "With this precious silver, I seal our union," he said, then dipped his finger into his jar. Silver paint dripped as he reached out to Ciara and smeared the paint all over her tuft of pubic hair, then between her legs. Ciara turned, bent, and Brenn did the same to her crack all the way down her slit.

Ciara stood, turned, and moved close to Brenn. She dipped her finger into her jar, and Erica saw shimmering gold paint dripping from it.

"With this precious gold, I seal our union." Ciara began to paint Brenn's pubic hair, then his cock. Erica expected him to have an erection, but it didn't happen. She watched as Ciara continued and painted his sack. Then Brenn turned and bent. Ciara ran her gold-dipped finger along his crack. The jars disappeared magically. The couple faced each other and held hands.

Though there wasn't a cloud in the sky, a flash of lightning came from above. A bright white light settled near Brenn and Ciara. Erica shielded her eyes. When she dared to look again, in the midst of that light stood the most ethereal image she could ever have imagined. It had to be Rania, the goddess of magick. She was beautiful beyond words. If angels existed, she surely was one. Brenn and Ciara now stood opposite each other holding hands. The goddess raised her hands. A melodious voice echoed throughout the valley. It almost seemed to bounce off the mountains surrounding it.

"Ciara, my child, you have now become the most powerful sorceress on Ierilia. With this union, you have received the last of your blessings. May you always use your magick with wisdom and for the good of the people. Brenn, my warrior, who I chose for this special princess, you have been given a great gift to be allowed to mate with Ciara. You will always protect her, guard her, and walk life's path with her, whatever it may bring."

The goddess stopped for a moment, held her hands up, and hundreds of tiny lights rained down on the couple.

"I now anoint you both. I bless this union, one such as Ierilia has never experienced. A lion and a dragon. May you be a formidable pair, both in battle and throughout life. Your path will be fraught with danger as you enter the future, but between you, you will be victorious of whatever the book of knowledge brings your way. Now go, my children. Let the waters of the Clyss cleanse you of any past iniquities and bless you for centuries to come. I will always watch over you and be there to guide you."

The voice drifted away. The light dissipated and with it, Rania. Brenn and Ciara, holding hands, walked into the waters of the Clyss.

Several people gasped. One uttered, "The monster that lurks below. They'll be killed."

King Biryn stood and held up his hands. "Please, quiet.

There is no monster in the lake. That monster was Ciara sleeping in the lake, where Cewrick held her captive. She would never have hurt anyone. It was our own fear that conjured up a terrible monster. They will reappear shortly. Just watch."

Laro squeezed her hand. Her libido now quieted, Erica realized suddenly that she'd held on to Laro's leg for dear life. She hadn't been so turned on in years, not since she'd become a widow. And really, she'd witnessed nothing erotic. It was their tradition and no sexuality was involved. She yanked her hand away and was beginning to wonder about Ciara and Brenn. They seemed to be underwater a long time. But then the tranquil surface moved, and Brenn and Ciara surfaced, still holding hands, the paint washed off their bodies. They smiled as they walked out and onto the beach and donned the silver and gold robes the women had left for them.

King Biryn approached them and embraced them both. Then he turned to the guests. "And now, there is another task I need to perform." He raised his hand, and a young man hurried to place a beautiful gold sword in the king's hands, much like his own.

"Captain Erica Martinez, please approach."

Erica stiffened. She glanced at Laro, then looked at the king again. Her? He wanted her to stand in front of all these people? Aldis nudged her.

Erica stood up hesitantly and slowly approached the king.

"For all your bravery and assistance in helping to find Icaras and to defeat Cewrick, I would like to present you with this special sword and offer you a commission of captain in my army. This will be written in the history records — that Erica Martinez from the planet Earth is the first female to serve in the king's army."

Erica had no choice but to take the sword. It was heavy, and she had to use all her might not to stumble with it as it

9

rested on her hands. It was also beautiful, almost equal to Brenn's sword.

"Thank you," she uttered, tongue-tied.

"You may think about it," the king said softly. "I had no other way to express my gratitude for your role in all that has happened. I will have special uniforms sewn for you."

Brenn grinned, patted her on the shoulder, then waved at the guests. "And now off to the feast that awaits us at my estate!"

CHAPTER TWO

"That was fucking awesome," Erica said as she sat behind Aldis in the flyer, carefully placing the sword next to her.

"I don't understand," Aldis said.

"I'm sorry. I am so impressed that my Earth language surfaced. It means that I am overwhelmed by that ceremony."

Aldis chuckled. "I'm sure that your Earth language will cause some questions. But I think that in the future some of it may drift into our language. Was this ceremony so different from the ones on Earth? How does a couple become united there?"

"Oh, it is so much different. Hard to explain. This ceremony is a cross between medieval and fantasy. If I were to describe this ceremony to anyone on Earth, they would think I was quoting something from a book."

"We have arrived at Brenn's estate. The feasting will continue throughout the night. What I am most grateful for is that Zohmes didn't interfere with the ceremony. I was afraid of that," Aldis unstrapped himself and stood up from his seat.

Erica nodded. "After the shocking ending of the betrothal feast, I agree. Do you think that Zohmes has given up?"

"No. I am sure that we are facing a lot more upheavals. He wants Cewrick released, but even if we wanted to, which we do not, we are not in a position to do that, and he knows it. I believe that he thinks if he harasses us enough, the gods and goddesses will give in and release the sorcerer."

"Would they ever give in?"

"No. Never. Cewrick is banished for all eternity. But meanwhile, we face Zohmes' wrath. Come. Let us go and feast."

As Erica walked to the house, followed by her crew, she couldn't help but think of the earthquake that had hit the night of the betrothal feast. What if that happened again? Sure, Ciara said she and Icaras had blocked Zohmes from sending another quake, but for how long? She looked at the parked flyers and the carriages. There had to be hundreds of people present.

Still deep in thought, she entered the great room to be greeted by Dunmore. "Captain, you look beautiful."

Erica smiled at him. After the way the betrothal party had ended, the lieutenant was providing extra security for the wedding celebration. "Thanks. Though I hate wearing dresses. It is so not me."

Laro walked up beside her and chuckled. "If it were up to me, you would wear nothing else."

Dressed in a dark blue tunic, edged in gold thread, black pants and boots, she had to admit Catrice was correct. The man was hot. All she could think about was sinking her fingers in his silky brown hair and tasting his kiss again.

"Yeah, right. Did you hear what the king offered me?"

"Yes. A commission in his army. Are you going to take it?"

"I'm very tempted, but I have to deal with my crew as well. Some of them don't seem to be comfortable living on Ierilia."

"Do you know the king has offered Ivran and me a commission as well?"

"Now how would I know that? I don't have the king's ear," she snapped, instantly regretting her biting remark. For some reason Laro managed to bring out the worst in her. Why? He was kind, eager to help her. Deep down she knew why. His touch set her blood on fire, his gaze caused her heart to go into overdrive.

"I'm seriously thinking about accepting. My life as a trader was rather dull."

"What would Tomas think of that? And who's going to take care of him while you are off to war?"

"We don't have a lot of war on Ierilia. The rewards are better, and while home, I will take care of Tomas, like always. You forget something. He's not a baby anymore. The main war we are facing right now is Zohmes, and I would want to be part of that anyway. Except, if I am an officer in the king's army, I will get paid for it."

"That makes sense. What about Ivran? Has he made up his mind?"

"I don't know. He had to discuss it with his mate."

"Well, I'll have to give it a lot of thought. Maybe if my crew can be given commissions, they'll feel differently. They're tired of being in the background."

"You need to speak to the king and maybe to Brenn about that."

"Meanwhile, I'm starving. I want to tackle some of that delicious food I saw on the tables."

Laro held his arm out to Erica and smiled. "Come, my lady. Let me escort you to the buffet tables."

Erica laughed at his antics and allowed him to take her arm. "Why of course, m'lord, lead the way. This wench could use some nourishment."

As they made their way to the tables laden with food, Erica began to relax. When she was with her crew, she had to constantly be the leader, but with Laro, she was an equal. His medieval ways could sometimes drive her bonkers, but during their missions, she did have fun rattling his cage. Several children were seated at a table, nibbling sweet cakes and fruit and sipping from glasses filled with milk. Erica had learned the milk came from an animal called a jago. One of the older children stood up, his big blue eyes alight with happiness as he rushed over to them. "Erica, you look so pretty!"

Erica pulled him into a hug. She didn't have to lean down to embrace him. At thirteen the boy was already taller than her 5'2" frame. "Thank you, Tomas."

"Well, you are," he said with a grin as he turned toward Laro. "Kira said we can camp in the orchard tonight, which Brenn said was fine."

Erica felt a twinge of pain at the softened look in Laro's eyes as he engulfed his son in a hug. She had that once, long ago, and it had been ripped away from her, her husband and child taken from her by the virus that had swept Earth. The government had given her a full dose of the vaccine so she would live and continue to serve in their military space program but lied to her when they gave her what she thought was the vaccine for her family. It was a placebo, meant to give her hope but also to keep her under their control. It had worked.

Laro reached out and clasped Erica's hand. "Are you all right?"

She forced the flashback from her mind and managed a smile. "Yeah, I'm fine. Just thinking of the past. Did Tomas leave?"

He gave her a searching look, gently squeezed her fingers, then released her hands. "He has joined the rest of the younglings. They are preparing to head out into the orchard to camp and play games. Come, let's get you fed."

Laro fixed a plate of cheeses, flat bread, sliced meats, and fruit while Erica grabbed two glasses of chairi fruit wine. She had tasted wine before at the dinner on Earth before she and her crew left on their mission. Erica didn't care for the wine they had served at the send-off party. It was heavy and made her feel like her cheeks had sucked completely inside her mouth, but the chairi fruit wine was pale pink, had a light fruity taste that wasn't too sugary, and the little bubbles made her want to giggle. She wasn't one to get drunk, but with the refreshing taste of this wine, she'd have to watch herself. She could drink too much of it very easily.

Erica joined Laro to walk out onto the balcony. He set the plate on one of the tables, pulled a chair out, and motioned for her to sit.

"Thank you, m'lord," she said and giggled. "This day really feels like I was sucked into a fantasy book. The ceremony was incredible, and I still can't get over how beautiful the sword is. It is so heavy I can barely hold it."

"Do you want to learn to wield it?"

"Who would teach me? Surely not Brenn. He doesn't have the time with being the king's general and just getting married."

"I could teach you. I may not carry a sword everywhere like Brenn, but I do own one, and I am trained to use it. The sword you were gifted was forged in Xynnar by my people. It is special because it has magical properties. The sword cannot break or be destroyed. The wielder of the sword will always strike true. The blade will never dull."

"Erica, Laro, we aren't disturbing you, are we?" Erica looked up to see Icaras, Laura, and Mark near the balcony entrance.

"No, please sit. We are just enjoying the quiet and the cool air," Laro said.

Mark placed a couple of wineskins on the table. "Chairi wine. Brenn's staff thinks of everything. Did you know he has stables on the grounds? He also produces most of the food that's served, right here on the estate, and they make their own wine."

"Is that common?" Erica asked. "I've seen little of the city yet, but I know the housing we were given seemed to be self-sustaining."

"It is common for the larger compounds, like where your crew is staying. Estates that have a large amount of land, like Brenn's, and if the owner can afford to hire staff to look after the grounds, grow their food, have livestock, and bring in very little from the markets. Any surplus is usually donated to hospitals, schools, and to those that need it," Laro said.

Laura twisted a lock of her blond hair around her finger. "Earth is so different. The government took control of everything. Whatever food they produced, they gave to the wealthy. Meat was unheard of. I had never tasted meat until our final dinner before take-off. They didn't care if people were starving. It was their way of culling the population."

Icaras took a sip of his wine. "Is that why you chose to join Erica's mission?"

"Yes, it is. I didn't actually choose. My sister and I volunteered. After a whole lot of tests, the government recruited us both and placed us with Erica. We all went through two years of training while the government was getting the spaceships ready. We wanted to leave Earth because we had no one. Our family had all died. My sister and I were alone. We were hoping to find a new life, and we have, I think. Even if it isn't the planet we were supposed to land on," Laura replied.

Erica looked at her two crew members. They had been through so much, both on Ierilia and Earth, but they seemed to be adjusting after their ordeal at Cewrick's castle. Looks could be deceiving, and Erica knew beyond a shadow of a doubt that Mark was still torn to pieces at the loss of his wife and unborn child. He was good at hiding it behind a quick smile. As her second-in-command, he put on a brave face in front of the crew, but here, where he could be more relaxed, she could see the pain in his eyes he tried to hide. Somehow, she needed to get Mark back into a role that would suit him. Anything to help him drown out the pain of losing Amanda.

"Why are you all hiding here? The feast is inside and in the courtyard."

Brenn's voice startled them. He and Ciara must have walked out onto the balcony while they were talking.

"Just catching a reprieve from all the noise and a breath of fresh air. Where are you two going on your honeymoon?" Erica asked.

"Honeymoon?" Ciara questioned.

"On Earth, when a couple unites, after the reception feast, they go away to be alone for a few days or weeks. Of course that tradition has become as extinct as meat. No one could afford to go away to a nice exotic island. So a honeymoon, when we left Earth, for the common people, was to spend a few days and nights together in a cheap hotel. Inn, or tavern, as you call it," Erica explained.

Brenn heaved a deep sigh. "There is little reprieve for us at this time. We have to plot a strategy to get rid of Zohmes. Icaras needs help in finding the other half of the amulet as told by Rania. In two days is Lord Quadra's trial by fire, for which I have to be present. Ciara and I will spend this night in the Clyss. We will be back before the suns rise."

"What a bummer. Maybe you can do the honeymoon later. Brenn, I need to ask you a question. Don't worry about it now, but I'd like to have an audience with the king. My crew is getting restless. They need to work, to keep busy. I hope you two at least enjoy your one night without any unwelcome interruptions," Erica said.

Laura smacked her on the arm. "Don't tempt fate. Or in this case, an angry god!"

"Don't be silly, Laura. Laro, I feel like dancing. You teach me some of your dances, and I'll teach you some Earth

17

moves."

It didn't escape her that Laro didn't need to be told twice. Up on his feet in a second, he took her hand and pulled her inside to head to the dance floor. The music played by the musicians almost sounded like a waltz. "This music on Earth would probably be called a waltz. Here, let me show you."

"You feel good in my arms," Laro said as he followed Erica's lead. She actually felt great but didn't answer him. In response, she placed both arms around his neck and rested her head against his shoulder. His arms tightened around her, and she moved against him seductively to the music. It had been so long since she'd been in a man's arms. It felt good. He felt good, and he was so damn sexy. She giggled as she envisioned him carrying her off to his room and making wild love to her.

"Erica, what is funny?" Laro said, speaking loudly to make himself heard over the music.

Erica giggled again. "Just me. I'm laughing at myself." Wriggling out of his arms, she pivoted and swayed to the music until she tripped and would have fallen if Laro hadn't caught her.

"Erica, my love, I think you've had too much chairi wine. It is a deceiving beverage because of its fruit taste. I'll take you to your room."

"Oooh, yes, please. Can you carry me?" She leaned against him and put her arms around his neck again. "Am I your love, Laro, my darling hero?"

"Hush. People are staring at us." Laro disengaged her clinging arms and, placing his arm around her waist, led her from the ballroom.

At her room, Erica opened the door, then beckoned him, pursing her lips and whispering, "Come, lover."

Laro caught her again as she tripped. He scooped her into his arms and carried her to the bed. Laying her down gently, he removed her sandals. "Oh yeah. I like... play... my feet..." she muttered and felt him take her into his arms. A dizzying wave hit her, and the room spun as if she was on a merry-go-round, then oblivion.

CHAPTER THREE

With a start, Erica woke up to full sunlight streaming into her room. "Damn. What time is it?" she muttered. She couldn't remember going to bed or at what time. The last thing she remembered was sitting on the balcony and talking to Brenn and Ciara.

That thought spurred her into action. Swinging her legs out of bed, she headed for the bathroom. After quickly bathing and getting dressed, she went to the kitchen. Brenn and Ciara had said they would be back before dawn.

She found almost everyone seated around the long, wooden kitchen table. Glad she wasn't the only one that had slept late, she greeted them. "Morning, everyone. Is it still morning?"

Laura laughed. "Yes. You're so used to getting up at the crack of dawn that to you this probably feels like lunchtime."

"Brenn, Ciara, welcome back from your one-night-stand." Erica noticed Brenn's raised eyebrows. "Sorry. That was an inappropriate comment. Your brief honeymoon."

"Since I don't know exactly what it means, I'll ignore it. Erica, you, Icaras, Aldis, Ciara, and I have an audience with the king this afternoon. He has requested us to join him in his private quarters," Brenn said.

"How did you know I wanted to speak to the king?" she asked.

Laro laughed. "What is the last you remember about last night?"

"Sitting on the balcony, drinking that delicious fruit wine and talking."

"You asked Brenn to arrange an audience with the king."

"Really? I don't remember that. I recall thinking about it."

Ciara giggled. "Erica, that wine is deceiving. It tastes like a fruit drink, but it is really much stronger than our regular wine. It is only served on special occasions."

"And I'm not much of a drinker. Haven't you noticed I only ever have one glass of what you call your regular wine, with lunch or dinner? It was warm in the house, and I drank quite a bit of that delicious fruity drink. I'll know now for future occasions to limit myself. I guess somewhere along the line I went to bed. Damn. I missed the rest of the party."

"It continued on into the wee hours of the morning," Laura said.

Erica thought she saw knowing looks between everyone and little snickers here and there. Maybe she was mistaken. Silently she hoped she hadn't made a fool of herself. Who could she ask? Even Laro gazed at her with a strange expression on his face. Grabbing a plate, she began to help herself to eggs, meat, and bread, then took the only empty seat by Laro.

Laro grinned at her and took a bite of the bread in his hand, carefully chewing, then swallowing the morsel. "Did you have sweet dreams, my lady?"

Erica glared at him. She was in no mood for Laro's games this morning. Her head pounded, her stomach was empty, and she hadn't even had a chance to drink a cup of coffee. "Ssshhhh... just hush. The sound of your voice is like a carpenter bee drilling a hole through my skull." She rubbed her forehead with her hand. Laro got up from the table and spoke to one of the kitchen staff. Before Erica knew what was going on, he returned to the table and pushed a warm cup into her hands.

"What is this?"

"Don't ask questions, just drink it. The herbs will ease your pain."

Erica tipped the cup to her lips and drank the warm liquid. It had a tart taste and reminded her of tea on Earth. She set the cup back down on the table. Within moments she felt a warming sensation throughout her body, and the incessant pounding in her brain eased. Looking up at Laro, she smiled in relief. "Thank you."

Laro pushed another steaming cup toward her. "I thought you'd want some coffee as well. Now eat. You have an audience with the king to attend."

Erica knew she really should try to curb his high-handedness, but she missed just being taken care of by someone else. As captain of the ship, she had no one else to turn to but herself.

"Brenn, are your parents leaving for Icaras' castle today?" Laro asked.

"They leave this afternoon. Some of our people have already moved there to help ready the castle and housing. The rest will arrive later in the week."

"I am thankful they are willing to handle matters for me while I adjust to the changes," Icaras said.

"Taking charge of any group of people is a daunting task, to say the least. You are a good man, Icaras. Your people already love you for freeing them. That's half the battle won." Erica gratefully sipped from her coffee.

She quickly finished her breakfast and stood up from the table. "I need to get a few things ready for my audience with the king."

Like Icaras, she had people to take care of, and she wanted to be prepared. The king would have a list of names and what their job title and duties were, but no one knew her crew better than she did. She would make sure her people were placed in areas they would love and not jobs they were forced into, as they had been on Earth.

"I'd like to assist if you don't mind, Erica. I know you're planning on asking the king to release us into the wilds of Ierilia. I can help with suggested job placements for the crew," Mark offered.

"I'd like that. Your input would make this easier. You can help me put some of the information together before my audience with the king. Let me go to my room quickly and retrieve my datapad. I'll meet you in the gardens. It's too nice a day to stay inside," Erica said as she headed to her rooms.

A weird sense of déjà vu overwhelmed her as she opened the door to her room. It was almost like a movie with no sound. Her pulling the come-hither look and beckoning to someone to follow her in. A stumble and strong arms that swept her up against a muscular chest, her head nestled against the man's shoulder. Damn, but it felt so good to be held like that. To be wanted. Her heart was pounding so hard in her chest she could barely breathe. Shaking her head to clear her vision, she stepped into her room and quickly shut the door. *Laro, what in the hell did we do last night?*

She leaned against the closed door for a few moments. Feelings that she hadn't felt since Rory now surfaced, flutters in her stomach, a need invading her loins. Resolutely, she shook her head and fetched her datapad. It amazed Erica just how generous the Ierilians were. The king had taken them under his wing, provided shelter, food, and clothing. Each member of her crew had been given a new datapad, translator, and communicator. "How am I ever going to repay his kindness?" she mused.

Erica turned on her datapad and smiled at the familiar information contained within it. Not only did she have access to all the information the Ierilians provided, but Rodriguez, her IT specialist, had managed to figure out how to convert the information on her laptop and copy it to her new datapad. The man was brilliant and could work on anything to do with computers and related equipment. She would suggest the king put Rodriguez on a team that would work to transfer the information from their ship's computers to Ierilian technology.

She left her room and knocked on Laura's door. After everything Laura had been through, Erica wanted her input before she suggested a job for the bright, young botanist. No answer, so she hurried back to the kitchen.

"Laura, can I speak with you for a moment?" she asked as she entered the kitchen.

Laura patted the chair beside her and poured a cup of what looked like tea for Erica. "Sure, I have plenty of time to talk."

Erica smiled. "I guess you do. How are you feeling? Do you feel up to starting a new job here? I wanted to consult with you before I talk to the king on your behalf."

"I like it here. The people have been so helpful and kind. The horrors I dealt with when Cewrick captured me and Mark don't overshadow the positives, but I don't think I am ready to deal with life outside of Brenn's estate yet. I feel safe here, protected. I know Julia would prefer if I returned to the compound to be with her, but I just can't," Laura said, her green eyes misting with tears.

Erica embraced Laura tightly, then pulled back and looked at her tearstained face. Laura was the youngest of their crew, a mere twenty, but had completed her degree in botany at an accelerated pace. Her sister Julia was six years older and tended to mother her. Not that Erica blamed her. Laura was all that she had left. "You are a strong woman, Laura. You wouldn't have been selected for the space relocation mission if you were not. We'll work through this together."

Not long after lunch, they joined the king in his private quarters. Erica was somewhat awed by the splendor of his rooms.

"Welcome. Please sit," Biryn told them, waving to comfortable chairs surrounding an ornately carved, of what looked like ivory, coffee table. A servant entered carrying a platter filled with golden goblets.

Erica suspected the contents to be wine and she was tempted to refuse, but did one really refuse a king's offering? She decided to take one but would merely sip from it.

"First I would like to hear from Erica. What can I help you with, Captain?"

Though the atmosphere was casual and relaxed, Erica felt far from it. "Your Majesty, my crew is becoming restless. They are tired of inactivity. I honestly think they have mastered enough of your language and customs and learned quite a lot about Ierilian history that they could be given suitable tasks."

The king chuckled. "Please, relax. Your request is reasonable. I will order my steward, Rilan, to consult with you. You have a list of your crew members and their experience?"

"Yes of course. I'll transfer the file to him after our meeting. You've already promoted me to captain in Brenn's army at the ceremony."

Biryn smiled. "Yes, I did say that because of your bravery alongside the men during the recent quests. But wouldn't you rather have a position in our space program?"

Erica shook her head. "A hovercraft and a flyer I can handle, but after our crash, I'd like to avoid space."

"Laro and Ivran have expressed the wish to join me as well," Brenn said.

"Brenn, I leave all that in your capable hands. Now let us discuss what you are going to do about Zohmes," Biryn said.

Ciara joined the conversation. "I heard from the goddess

Rania this morning. Before we deal with Zohmes, we need to help Icaras find the other half of his amulet. Rania told me an interesting story, one that could only be revealed now."

"That's why you were gone for a while when I woke up," Brenn said.

"Yes. Rania called out to me. When Icaras came into this world, he was not alone. There was another infant, a girl child. Cewrick killed the woman who helped with the birthing. Then he killed Hirsuta. Cewrick didn't want the second infant. He took her and threw her into the river beyond the Sucronian Mountains. The gods permitted Rania to intervene. She saved the infant before she fell into the raging current and placed her by a well-traveled road and rendered her invisible. Only the couple chosen by the gods to raise her could see or hear her. What happened to the infant after that, Rania doesn't know. She also told me that Icaras' sister will be an integral part of defeating Zohmes."

A perplexed look crossed King Biryn's face. "What does she have to do with Icaras' amulet?"

Icaras' eyes widened in amazement. "She is my sister, my twin! Of course, she would have the other half of the amulet. Our mother would have placed it around her neck as she did mine."

Biryn tapped his finger on the table. "You must find your sister. Then we can formulate a plan to defeat Zohmes. We will continue this discussion after you have the other half of the amulet. The search will have to wait until after Lord Quadra's trial by fire tomorrow. Brenn must be present. Go now, get some rest, tomorrow will be a long day."

After returning to Brenn's estate, Erica quietly walked out to the gardens and sat in the grass under the shade of a small tree. On Earth she hadn't been able to spend much time outdoors while training for the mission, and of course on the ship there was nothing but being in stasis until the crash had awakened them so rudely. Leaning against the tree, she tilted her head back to rest against the trunk and closed her eyes. The warmth of the suns' rays on her face made her smile. The sound of footsteps caused her to open her eyes.

"Erica?" Laro's deep voice rumbled behind her.

Erica's heart skipped a beat. The effect the man had on her was driving her insane. She just hadn't figured out if it was a good thing yet. "I'm over here, Laro. Hiding from you."

Laro sat down on the grass beside her and handed her a waterskin. "Why would you be hiding from me?"

A flash of memory, her moving seductively against Laro, her arms wrapped around his neck. *Ah, God! Surely, I didn't.*

Laro took her hand in his. "What's wrong, Erica?"

She looked up at those deep blue eyes of his. God, he was delectable. His dark brown hair framed an almost angelic face with full lips, a strong chin, and a dimple that made her go weak at the knees every time he smiled. "What exactly happened last night?"

Laro smiled at her, still holding her hand. "Nothing happened. You had a little too much wine, so I helped you to your room. You stumbled and almost fell, so I carried you to your bed, nothing more."

Erica squeezed his hand, then let go. Could she believe it was that simple? The flashes she was having were telling a different story. She really hoped she hadn't made a fool of herself. Not wanting to think about it anymore, she changed the subject. "Laro, why aren't you attending the trial?"

He searched her face as if he knew she was unsure of his answer. "It's a private event not to be witnessed by the general population, though the judgement will be recorded and the people notified of the outcome. The gods will be the judges. Only the king, several of his counsel, Brenn, Ciara, Icaras, and you are allowed to be there."

"Why does it have to be private? And if that's the case, how come I have to go?"

"An ordinary trial is held in the king's courtroom, and the king and his counsel are judge and jury. It is very seldom that the gods will act thus. Only if the crime is extreme will the gods be the judges. You were told to be there because you are the leader of the Earth people and you need to learn everything about our customs."

Erica took another drink from the waterskin. "Is there much crime on Ierilia? Besides those committed by sorcerers, of course. I mean, thievery, murder, arson, drug trafficking, and such."

Laro shook his head. "Not a lot. Our people want for nothing. Murder is a rare occurrence. There is no poverty on the planet. There is a drug made from bindweed. It is forbidden to make and sell it. And most are terrified of the punishment, especially if the gods are judge and jury. Though those trials are private, the people do know what happens during them."

"So are those trials all by fire if the gods are involved?"

"No, the methods vary according to the crime, but as I said, it happens so seldom."

"Is there a jail on Ierilia?"

"Jail?"

"A big building where murderers, thieves, and other criminals are sent for punishment. They can't leave that building. They have a cell with a barred locked door. They have to perform duties within the jail during the day, and they are only allowed on the grounds of it at certain times. The grounds are surrounded by high barbed wire fences and guards all around."

"No, there is no such place here except for the dungeons below the palace. Those are only used for a short period as the king will hold court and perform the sentencing quite fast. If

28

the king sentences someone for stealing, he or she is sent to work in the mines and has to live in a guarded compound. And as I said, crime is minimal on our planet."

"Wow. Well, the trial by fire tomorrow will be interesting, but I wish you could go along," Erica said wistfully.

CHAPTER FOUR

rica seated herself in Brenn's flyer and gazed out the window. "Where is the arena? Is it far?"

Brenn set the coordinates and turned to her. "Nothing is far using the flyer, but it is on the outskirts of the city."

"You know, that's another question that's been hanging in my mind. I've seen no cars. Are there any vehicles on Ierilia?"

"Cars?" Ciara asked.

"Let me show you." Erica opened her datapad and brought up some pictures of cities on Earth. She handed it to Ciara.

"Your cities look very busy," Brenn said, looking at the photo with Ciara.

"They are. Do you see those metal cars?"

"Yes. I see metal transport machines in various shapes and colors. Many of them. We have nothing like that. The people on large estates have a flyer. We all have horses. Farmers use carts drawn by horses to carry their wares to markets. Some people have carriages, as you saw the night of the feast. People that live within the city walk to most destinations."

"It's probably a good thing. Those cars give off a lot of carbon dioxide emissions and are one of the causes of the polluted atmosphere. We also have busses, large vehicles that transport a lot of people, airplanes, and trains. We also ride bicycles and other methods of transportation. Just flip through the photos, and you'll see more pictures."

"What a beautiful baby. Who is she?" Ciara said and held the datapad up.

Erica swallowed the lump that formed instantly in her throat. "That was my little girl. Her name is Marina."

Ciara took Erica's hand and squeezed it, her violet eyes filled with concern. "I am so sorry. I've made you sad. She is so pretty and looks like you."

"My government did that to me. If they had given my husband and baby the vaccine, they would be alive today."

Ciara tucked a stray lock of hair behind her ear. "And you might not be here now. You most probably would have chosen to stay on Earth with your mate and daughter. The gods had different plans for you, Erica. Marina is safe in the realm of dreams now."

"The people on Earth believe in one God. Your gods don't watch over Earth. Maybe each universe has its own deity or in your case, multiple deities."

"One day you will hold your baby again," Ciara murmured softly.

Erica fidgeted with the seat straps. "Ciara, I know you mean well, but I don't believe in reincarnation. Can we change the subject? Are we almost there?"

"Yes, we're about to land," Brenn said.

Erica followed Icaras, Brenn, and Ciara out of the flyer. As she stepped off the last tread, she gasped. It was as if she were looking at a Greek or Roman arena, except the one in front of her wasn't historical. It looked in pristine condition. "What else is the arena used for?"

"Games and our yearly festival."

Erica wondered what kind of games but didn't have time to ask as they entered the arena. Brenn led them to a platform. The king and his entourage were already seated. "Your Majesty," Erica greeted and bowed her head.

There were seats ready for them behind the king and his

counsel. Erica sat and looked down at the circle of sand. About ten feet above it the bleachers began. In her imagination she saw chariots racing. Then her mind drifted to another old movie in which gladiators had to fight each other. As she gazed at the arena, large metal circles, slightly taller than a man, appeared from the ground, evenly spaced. They were all the same size except for one. It was directly in front of them and larger. Doors opened beneath the bleachers. Two guards appeared. Between them, in chains, stood a man wearing nothing but a loincloth. He was tall and muscular with a not-unpleasant face. His shoulder-length brown hair looked unkempt and wild.

The guards led him to stand directly in front of the large ring below the king.

Erica watched in awe as Biryn stood, a gold scepter in his hand. He was dressed in royal finery, a deep blue cloak falling off his shoulders, his golden sword strapped to his side. The blue of his tunic brought out the vivid color of his eyes and contrasted against his hair that had been braided on both sides. A gold crown perched on his head. She thought him very handsome with his Viking good looks and piercing blue eyes, though he couldn't compare to Laro...

"How do you plead, Lord Quadra?"

"Not guilty, Your Majesty."

Clouds appeared above the arena, but when Erica gazed closer, it was more like a vapor, a mist.

"The gods have made their presence known. You may speak in your defense," Biryn told the man, who continued to stare at the ground instead of facing the king.

"Your Majesty, it was Klubotah. He invaded my lands. I had no choice but to defend what has belonged to my family for generations."

"Your testimony will be judged by the gods. If you have spoken with a true tongue, the fire will tell us that we have wrongfully captured you. Let it begin."

"Your Majesty, please—"

"Silence, or I will order your tongue removed!"

The guards removed the chains and stepped back when suddenly the circles burst into flame, the fire reaching the center of each circle. Erica felt almost sorry for the man as he tried to run away, but the guards pushed him forward.

"Now what?" Erica softly asked Icaras, who sat next to her.

Icaras brushed his dark hair out of his eyes. "If he speaks the truth, the flames will be cold. If he lies, the flames will burn him. After each circle, he still has a chance to speak the truth. If he doesn't, the fire will slowly eat at him as he passes through each."

Erica shivered. *What a harsh way to die.* "What happens if he speaks the truth and admits his guilt?"

"He will still be punished, but his punishment won't be as severe. The longer he waits to speak, the harsher his punishment becomes. If he had confessed when the king asked him to speak in his own defense, the gods might have been lenient and sent him to the mines for the remainder of his life."

The man stepped through the first ring. He didn't utter a sound. Neither did he speak when he crossed the space to the second ring, but she thought she could see blisters on his arms and legs. So that showed he had been lying. The man made it through the fifth circle, his body now severely blistered. Erica doubted he could make it through the other circles until the last one. But he was strong and continued. Each time he walked through a wall of fire, he screamed as the flames seared him. He finally came to the last, the taller circle. A rumbling sounded from above. The man was at the point of collapse, his hair almost burned off his head, blisters on his scalp. He stood gazing at the circle, refusing to move into the wall of flame facing him. He fell to the ground, on his knees.

The two guards rushed to his side and pulled him up to stand straight. Even if he spoke now, Erica knew he'd not survive what looked like third-degree burns. The guards pushed him forward into the raging fire.

Erica clenched her hands as his screams tore through the arena. The fire turned green, then blue, and finally a bright red. All the circles were once again just bright metal shining in the sunlight. The foggy mist was gone. So was the man. The last circle had incinerated him completely.

"I guess he was guilty as sin," Erica said.

Brenn nodded. "I knew that since I was the one who brought him in. But because he kept maintaining his innocence, he was given a last chance to speak the truth and confess. Perhaps the gods might have been merciful and sentenced him to the mines although I sincerely doubt it. His treachery caused the death of many brave Ierilians."

"What is another punishment, besides death?"

"Garissa Island. It is a fate almost worse than death. Any that have been judged by the trial by fire have usually made it no further than the second circle. They confessed and were sent to Garissa Island. There have not been many."

After the king and his counsel left, they headed back to the flyer. Erica strapped herself in. "When does the search for Icaras' sister begin?"

"Tomorrow," Icaras said.

"We leave for the river at sunup. Our search will begin there," Ciara told her.

Brenn turned to her. "First we will look for the road Rania mentioned. We will come across villages, and we'll need to question people, show them Icaras' amulet and ask if they know anyone that has one like it."

"It's like looking for a needle in a haystack." Erica sighed.

"What does that mean?" Ciara asked.

"Mm, hay is what we put in the animal stables on Earth.

It's like dried grass. You've got it. I've seen it in your stables."

"Oh, you mean drunga grass," Brenn told Erica.

"Imagine a tall stack of that with a needle somewhere inside it and having to find that needle."

"Almost impossible." Ciara grimaced.

"Exactly."

"The goddess will guide us," Icaras said.

"I hope so. Let's hope Zohmes keeps his cool," Erica muttered.

Erica hadn't realized that the afternoon had almost passed. It was nearly dinnertime. Her stomach growled as they approached the house and she smelled the aroma of barbecued meat. She'd never noticed the stone barbecue pit at the edge of the courtyard. Smoke billowed from it.

"I see the cook is smoking a Zangoona bird," Brenn said while inhaling the scent.

"Zangoona? It looks huge, almost like a turkey, except bigger. I'm starving. By the way, are we allowed to talk about the trial and execution? There will probably be questions from my crew."

Brenn gave her a piercing stare. "That is why the king asked you to attend. Crime is taken very seriously, and the punishments can be harsh as you have seen. Your crew members are integrating into our world and will be treated the same as Ierilians should they commit a crime. They need to understand this."

Erica nodded. After what she had seen at the trial she had to make sure her people understood the ramifications if they transgressed. "I'll make sure they understand. I'll tell them everything I've learned today."

"Come, Geith has prepared a feast, and my stomach is empty after such a long day."

They continued into the house and walked into the dining

hall. The room was empty of both people and food. The doors leading out to the courtyard were open. Erica could see lights flickering outside, and the sounds of voices and laughter filled her ears.

"The staff has set a table for us outside." Brenn headed for the wide open doors to the balcony.

Erica followed Brenn and Ciara out to the courtyard. The staff had set up a long table surrounded by netting. Flower garlands braided with twinkling lights draped from the top of the netting down the side. Tiny lights also flickered throughout the top of the netting, reminding Erica of the stars above them. Mark and Laura were seated at the table with Ivran and his mate, Reana, little Issa seated in her lap, gurgling happily. Laro and Kira stood off to the side with Tomas, a scowl darkening his face.

"But I don't want to go to that castle. Shanina said she was coming back here to stay with Brenn," Tomas argued.

Erica couldn't be sure, but it looked like the boy's hair was growing longer and getting coarser, his limbs and face changing. Suddenly, with a cry that turned into a growl, Tomas' whole body changed from the thirteen-year-old boy she knew into a young lion with a bewildered expression in his eyes. The lion shook his head and took first one shaky step, then another, before stopping. He finally dropped to the ground to rest on his stomach. He opened his mouth making a sound that almost sounded like a squeak instead of a lion's snarl.

Laro rushed to Tomas and kneeled beside him, rubbing his fur. "It's okay, son. I know you're scared." He leaned toward Tomas, hugged him close, then looked up, catching Erica's gaze.

The concern in his eyes wrenched at Erica's heart. Without thinking, she rushed to Laro.

Laro grasped her hand in his and squeezed. "I hadn't told

him yet that his shifting ability would come naturally now and to fear it no longer. He has been warned from birth not to shift because he would lose his humanity."

Ciara giggled and walked up to Tomas, patted his head, and said, "I hated my adolescent years. Every time your mood swings one way or the other, poof. We held school outdoors because of this." She kneeled in front of Tomas, still petting him. "Don't be frightened, Tomas. Just think of your human body wearing clothing, and you'll change right back."

"Is that how you dragons do it? Meanwhile, you just let me get naked every time I shifted?" Brenn asked Ciara.

"Maybe I just like seeing you get naked." She grinned up at him cheekily.

Erica laughed at the couple's word sparring and glanced at Tomas. As quickly as he had shifted into a lion, his human form appeared, fully clothed, his thin body shaking, his eyes filled with fear.

Tomas leaned his head against Laro's chest, and to Erica's surprise, the boy had a death grip on her hand. "I'm sorry, Father. I didn't mean to do that. I don't like it. It felt strange."

Laro hugged his son close one more time and stood, helping a still-shaking Tomas to his feet, then reached down and grasped Erica's hand to help her. "Thank you, Erica." Turning to his son, he ruffled the boy's hair. "Thank the gods the curse has been removed. Come on, sprout, let's go eat."

Every glance of those blue eyes, each touch of his hand, crumbled the walls she'd built to keep him at a distance. How was she going to fight the invisible pull between them? Did he feel it, too? Erica took a deep breath to still the fast beat of her heart and joined them at the table. Laro pulled a chair out for her to sit down, then took a seat beside her, Tomas seated on her other side. The scalded area of her heart flared and intensified. This was how it should have been with her husband and daughter. Steeling herself against the feelings he evoked, Erica looked up to drink in the beauty of their enchanted setting.

Brenn's staff moved quickly around the table, filling glasses of mead for the adults and jago milk for Tomas, then placed platters of sliced Zangoona bird, roasted gana root, sliced wraggia fruit, soft cheese, and loaves of crusty bread on the table.

Erica took a drink from her glass and glanced up at Mark and Laura.

"Did he just..." Mark said.

"That was incredible! Just like the shapeshifter books from home!" Laura exclaimed at the same time.

"Brenn and the people from Xynnar are all lion shifters. Like my people, they were cursed. Now that the curses are broken, they can shift at will," Ciara explained.

"It looked like Tomas was able to shift much easier than Brenn did the first time." Laro placed slices of the smoked meat and vegetables on Erica's plate before serving himself.

Erica caught the pointed look and grin Laura gave her. She knew she shouldn't allow Laro to continue trying to take care of her, but the man was stubborn. She had to admit to herself that deep inside she craved the caring he so easily gave. She couldn't help but compare him to Rory. He had been a good husband, but they had been really independent of each other. It was almost as if they had lived separate lives. She couldn't imagine Rory ever dishing up a plate of food for her.

Ciara continued to explain. "Though a shifter's natural state is their human body, we were born to shift. Because of the curse, the lion was kept dormant until the young ones reached puberty. As young men and women, they had to fight to gain control of their lion half to keep from shifting. The forced containment of the natural ability to shift is what causes the pain in adults the first time. The young ones will experience no pain."

"This place is special in so many ways I could never have dreamed. Is the ability to shift magic?" Laura asked.

Ciara nodded. "In many ways, it is."

"Speaking of magic, how are we going to track down an amulet that belongs to an invisible woman?" Erica said.

Icaras rubbed his chin thoughtfully. "I have had some time to think about how we will find her. When we are born, our souls are tied at first to our parents, then later to family, then to our closest friends. Eventually, if we are lucky enough to find him or her, the strongest tie is to our lifemate. My soul is tied to my sister's. It has to be. No matter how weak that connection is, I will sense it. That bond will help us find her."

"On Earth, some people believe twins are born with a bond that ties them together. That they can sense things about the other, like if one is injured the other will feel the pain. Is this something like you are suggesting?" Mark asked.

Pain darkened Icaras' gray eyes. "Yes, I believe it is. I was cursed with feelings of an emptiness, insecurity, and inadequacy while I was still young, before Cewrick changed me into the worm, never knowing I had a twin sister. I could feel an aching pull toward something. I always thought it was the loss of my mother that caused this. Now I know it had to be my sister. She has always been with me. I just had no idea she existed for me to look for her."

"We will find her, Icaras. Somehow, we will find her," Brenn said.

After dinner, Erica stood in the garden, looking up at the clear night sky. She needed to get some rest. Aldis would be picking them up well before sunrise, but she had just finished arranging assignments for some of her crew. Catrice, the ship's doctor, Jason, a lab technician, and Jill, as well as the other nurses, were assigned to the hospital in Cront. Security personnel was given the option to join the space fleet or the ground warriors. Some of her crew were farmers or carpenters. Each person was placed according to the skill they had been trained for on Earth.

Erica had felt the tension and unease coming from a couple of her crew. She understood how hard it was to settle in a new place, how hard it was to trust in a government entity, but the king and the Ierilians were being more than accommodating to her crew. She just wished they would all simply accept their destiny. *I'll have to sit down and talk with those that are showing resentment and anger at the hand fate has dealt them.*

Sitting down on a stone bench near a fish pond in the center of the garden, Erica took her datapad out of her bag and sent her acceptance of the assignments to King Biryn's steward. She placed the datapad back into her bag and walked to her room. Opening the door, she placed her bag on the bed and headed to the bathroom. She turned on the water to fill the deep tub, quickly undressed, and stepped into the soothing water, hoping to relax enough to sleep. She grabbed the scented soap the staff stocked the bathrooms with and worked up a lather, then washed and rinsed. After pulling the plug out, she grabbed a towel, quickly wrapped herself in it, and walked back into her room to grab a shirt to sleep in.

A light knock sounded at her door as she donned the shirt and vigorously dried her short hair with the towel. "Come in," she called out as she dropped the towel on a chair and worked at taming her unruly curls with her fingers.

Laro entered the room and quietly shut the door. His gaze seared her as he looked her from head to toe and back. Her freshly scrubbed, flushed skin felt feverish, her heart pounding so hard against her ribs, she was sure he could hear it. Liquid heat pooled in her belly, and she could feel the dampness of her arousal between her thighs.

Laro held out a large package. Whatever was inside was wrapped in cloth. "I brought something for you. I thought you might like it."

Erica reached out to take the package but suddenly found herself pulled against his muscular chest, the package falling to the floor. "Gods, woman, you are driving me crazy," he said, then lowered his head and captured her lips in a scalding kiss.

Erica felt herself melt against him, the walls in her mind and heart she had tried so desperately to repair at dinner crumbling around her. She wrapped her arms around his neck and opened her mouth to the teasing assault of his teeth and tongue. His hands scalded her skin as they slowly traveled down her back to slide under her shirt. He grasped the round cheeks of her ass, lifting her so she could wrap her legs around his waist.

Breaking the kiss, Laro caught her gaze and slowly walked them to her bed. Erica gasped as the hard ridge of his cock rubbed against her core, the delicious friction driving her mad. Carefully, Laro set her down on top of the comforter and came down on top of her, caging her body beneath his, then lowered his head and nipped her lower lip.

Erica wound her arms around him, gliding her hands beneath the material of his tunic. *Fuck the ramifications.* For once she just wanted to let go, to take what the man offered and give of herself in return. She grabbed the hem of his tunic, aching to feel every inch of those muscles beneath her fingers. "Take off your shirt."

Laro gazed down at her, eyes blazing. "Will you let me remove yours?" he asked as he shifted to his side beside her and ran his fingers lightly from her knee, up the inside of her leg, to the slick wetness at the apex of her thighs. He grabbed the base of her shirt, his hand brushing her skin as he slowly tugged it upward, exposing the soft flesh of her stomach.

Erica felt like she was doused in ice water as Donna's voice sounded over her communicator. "Captain, this is Donna. I'm sorry to bother you so late, but we need to talk."

Laro's hand stilled on her stomach as Erica pulled her shirt down, sat up, and grabbed the communicator. "Give me a few minutes, and I'll call you back."

She stood up from the bed, rubbing her face with her hands. How could she have let this go so far? She had a crew to worry about, people to take care of. Strong arms encircled her from behind, her stiff back pulled against Laro's chest. God how she wanted to just lean into his strength, but she couldn't let herself get involved with him, no matter how he made her feel. Turning in his arms, she looked up into those deep blue eyes. "Laro, I can't do this, whatever *this* is. It can't, no... it *won't* happen," she said as she pushed at his chest.

Erica gasped as Laro suddenly let her go, his pain-filled gaze boring into her before quickly going blank, a wall successfully building between them. "As you wish, my lady," he said as he made his way to the door and walked out of her room.

Erica clutched her chest. Her heart felt as if it had just been ripped in two, a vital part of herself missing. A shudder wracked her body as she braced herself against the pain, then turned and grabbed the communicator off the table. "What did you need, Donna?"

"You were with him again, weren't you, *Captain*? Don't try to deny it. Well, while you were playing with the native, we already handled the situation," Donna said.

Erica took a deep breath and let it out slowly, guilt hammering at her because she knew Donna was right, but anger took its place at the tone Donna had taken with her. "That is enough, Lieutenant. I'm not even going to ask what situation you're referring to. If something else comes up, call me. *I* will personally handle it." She closed the communicator and dropped it to the floor.

Looking down, her attention was caught by the package

Laro had brought her. She grabbed it from the floor, sat on her bed, and pulled the ties that kept the material closed around it. The soft cloth fell open. Inside was a scabbard with scrolling design work etched into the leather to match the sword the king had given her. Erica traced the pattern with her fingertip as the pain that ripped her apart threatened to suffocate her. Curling to her side on the bed, clutching the scabbard against her chest, she cried for the first time since losing her husband and daughter.

Laro leaned against the closed door of Erica's room, shutting his eyes as pain engulfed him. His beautiful lifemate was fighting the bond between them every step of the way. He had only meant to give Erica the scabbard he'd asked Kira to make, but the moment he saw her, damp from her bath, the scent of her arousal filling the air, need had clamped him like a vice. He had yearned to taste the sweetness of her lips again. The kiss they had shared in the caverns had sealed his fate. His soul was hers, and he had realized then that the gods had sent this woman to him — that she was his true lifemate. Erica had no idea of the special gift the gods had given them, had no idea what they were to each other. It shattered a part of him to close himself off, to stifle the connection between them, but to keep his sanity there was no other way. Her love for her crew, the anguish of losing her husband and child, every emotion she felt, blazed a path straight to his soul. They had a mission to complete and a god to banish. This distraction could get them all killed.

The sound of her crying reached him through the closed door. Taking a deep, shuddering breath, he fought the urge to rush inside and hold her close to ease her suffering. He knew she would push him away. For all her hidden softness, she had an unforgiving strength and refused to show weakness in front of others, especially him. Steeling himself against the turmoil that battered him, he left her door and quietly walked to his room.

CHAPTER FIVE

Erica woke much earlier than she'd intended. Her night had been restless, plagued by dreams of what had occurred between her and Laro the previous evening. She'd also had dreams about Donna, John, Jill, and several other of her crew that had shown some rebellion. Dreams? They were more like nightmares.

The first opportunity she had, she needed to talk to her crew and address these issues. Right now, there was no time as they were to leave at sunrise to help Icaras find the missing amulet and his sister. "What an impossible fucking task," she muttered as she washed, then got dressed. "An invisible woman wearing an invisible amulet. Right. Let's go and start spraying paint around into thin air. The girl could be anywhere on this fucking planet."

Angrily, she struggled with the sword and scabbard. "Get a grip on yourself, woman," she hissed as she threw the offending items onto the bed.

Still in turmoil, she decided to head for the kitchen. Coffee would taste really good right then, and the kitchen staff would already be getting breakfast ready.

To her surprise, she found Laro already seated at the kitchen table, reading from his datapad. Her heart skipped a beat or two at the sight of him. Squashing her turbulent feelings, she mumbled a good morning.

Laro placed the datapad on the table. "Good morning, Erica. All ready and eager to start this mission?"

How can he sit there calm and collected and exchange pleasantries after what happened between us last night? She nodded. "Yes, eager to get these quests behind us so that we can live normal lives."

"After Aldis flies us to the other side of the Sucronian Mountains, Ciara will lead us to the spot at the river where the goddess saved the infant and the road she placed her beside. Where is your sword, Erica? This will not be as dangerous a mission, but we still need weapons. Much of it we'll travel on horseback, and there are dangerous predators living in the forests we may need to pass through."

"Where will we get horses? They'll be waiting for us beside the river?" she said sarcastically.

"Erica, come here."

"No."

"Please?"

Hesitantly, she sat beside him. "I need coffee." She'd spoken loud enough, and one of the cook's helpers quickly brought her a mug filled to the brim. Greedily she drank from it.

"I apologize for my behavior last night." Laro spoke very softly so that the kitchen staff couldn't hear. "I overstepped the boundaries. I've been without a woman for many years and you are more than desirable. I beg your forgiveness for my presumptuousness in thinking you wanted me as much as I wanted you."

It was as if he'd driven a knife straight into her heart. But isn't this what she wanted? To strengthen that wall between them? Had he merely wanted to screw her? She steeled herself. "Don't worry about it. My reasons were much like yours. Friends?"

Laro nodded. "Friends. Now, about the sword —"

"The scabbard is beautiful, thank you, but I couldn't strap the damn thing on. And before I wield a sword, I need some lessons."

"I'll help you strap it on, and there'll be plenty of time while we're traveling for us to teach you. When we make camp in the evenings, for instance."

"You're both up early. What's this about camp in the evenings?" Brenn asked as he sat at the table.

"Erica needs lessons in wielding her new sword."

"Yes, we can teach her when we make camp, though we may spend the nights in the inns in some of the villages we'll pass through," Brenn said.

"Laro said we'll be on horseback."

"Yes. After we find the road, we'll travel it on foot until we can buy horses and supplies. I looked at the map, and the first village, Xandero, is not that close to the mountains. We need to carry enough food in our backpacks to last at least two days, although if need be, we can always hunt. I have already instructed the cook to ready traveling packs for us all. Pack your bedroll and a change of clothing. Make sure you bring a warm jacket, Erica. We are getting closer to winter and the nights are getting colder, especially on the other side of those mountains."

The kitchen staff began placing platters of eggs, leftover smoked meat from the night before, bread, fruit, and pastries on the table. Erica's stomach rumbled loudly.

Laro chuckled. "I think someone is hungry."

She helped herself to a generous amount of the delicious smoked meat and the bread. She toyed with the food on her plate. "I don't trust that Zohmes character. He showed us his fury, and since then it's been calm and quiet. Like the calm before the storm at sea."

"I have had the same thought," Brenn agreed.

"We will have to keep our guard up. I have no doubt he

will use any tool at his disposal," Laro said.

Erica slid her half-eaten plate of food away. The dreams from the night before still plagued her. "I need to go grab my gear and speak to Mark before we leave." She pushed her chair away from the table and left the kitchen. Halfway to her room, she ran into Mark, Laura, and Icaras on their way to the kitchen. "Mark, can I talk to you a moment?"

"Of course." Mark turned to Icaras and Laura. "Save me some coffee!"

"We can talk on the way to my room. I have to grab a few things."

Mark fell in step beside Erica. "What's on your mind, Captain?"

"Captain? When have you ever called me captain in private?"

Mark glanced at her and shook his head. "From the moment I noticed you are wearing your captain's hat. Seriously, Erica, what's going on?"

Erica stopped in front of her door, opened it and motioned for Mark to enter. "First, while I am on this mission, I'm going to need you to oversee the assignments for the crew. I sent my approval to the king's steward last night. He knows to contact you if he has any questions. You should have a copy of the assignments and my approval waiting for you."

"I was already prepared to handle that while you were away. Now, tell me what's really bothering you."

Erica sat on the bed and motioned for Mark to sit by her. "I'm leaving you in charge of the crew. Several of them are unhappy about our situation. Some have been rebellious, and I'm worried they may do something stupid and possibly offend our hosts. I'd like to keep that from happening and want all of our people to be safe and happy."

"You can count on me. I'll keep them in line and safe until you return."

"Thank you, Mark. Now I should grab my stuff and head down to the courtyard. I don't want to keep them waiting."

Mark stood and walked to the door, grabbed the handle, then turned to look back at her. "Erica, you *are* allowed to be happy, too." He winked, then walked out, shutting the door behind him.

Erica leaned against one of the trees in the courtyard, her pack on the ground by her feet and the sword and scabbard resting on top. She had given up trying to strap the convoluted thing onto her back. There were way too many straps for her to deal with and not enough caffeine in her system.

She looked up as the sounds of footsteps and voices disturbed the quiet morning. Ivran, Laro, and Icaras walked toward her, their packs in their hands. Both Ivran and Laro had swords strapped to their backs. Brenn and Ciara were behind them, holding hands, lost in their own little world of love and romance. Erica felt bad that their romantic getaway had to be cut short by a mission to find Icaras' sister — and to best an angry god with a vendetta against the planet.

Laro joined her by the tree and dropped his pack on the ground beside hers. "Good. You remembered to bring your sword and scabbard," he said as he reached down to pick up the scabbard. "Come here. I'll adjust it for you and show you how to wear it."

Laro helped her into it, then adjusted the straps to fit her shoulders. The brush of his fingers against her neck seared her skin. Her pulse raced as his hands moved to her waist, adjusting and securing the strap there. Her body really wasn't in tune with her mind. Somehow, she was going to have to figure out how to get her raging hormones in check, or this was going to be a very long mission.

Laro stepped back. "All you have to do now is release the

waist strap and slip the harness off your shoulders to remove it."

Erica just wanted to grab his shoulders and shake him. Her body ached to continue what they had started the night before, and he was Mr. Calm, Cool, and Collected. "Thank you."

She glanced at the horizon. The rising suns had painted the sky multiple shades of purple, orange, and yellow. Shielding her eyes from the bright rays, she caught sight of Aldis' hovercraft.

The wind kicked up and ruffled her short curls as the craft landed in the courtyard. Grabbing her pack from the ground, she followed the group in through the open door and took the seat beside Laro. Of course, that would be the only empty one. It was like the planet's forces were conspiring against her. From the moment they'd met at the crash site, she had been drawn to him like a moth to an open flame—first because of his easy smile and quick friendship, then because of the tender way he handled his son. When he'd kissed her in the caverns and claimed her as his, he had awoken a part of her she never knew existed. Not even Rory had ignited such fire within her. She *wanted* to be claimed by him. Wanted it so badly it made her ache, and damned if she didn't want to stake a claim on him, too. What stopped her? It wasn't as if she was still a virgin. What she felt, was it merely lust? Laro had told her he'd been alone for a long time. So had she. But she had never believed in casual sex, like so many of her friends engaged in. An affair could easily kill a friendship. Hell, just the short interaction they'd had already caused a change in their relationship.

She glanced up at the subject of her obsession. Normally Laro would be talking to her, describing the towns, scenery, and local customs. He was always so attentive and easygoing. Today he sat leaning back in the seat, his head resting against the wall of the hovercraft, eyes closed, completely oblivious to the emotions he stirred within her. So much for the whole *you are mine* claim.

"I decided to let Dunmore pilot. I'm hoping, once we accomplish what we've set out to do, he can come and fetch us. It will save a considerable amount of time. We should reach the other side of the Sucronian Mountains shortly. There is a valley by the river where he can land the hovercraft. From there, we go on foot until we reach Xandero," Aldis informed them.

Erica was so deep in thought that his voice startled her. *Damn. I need to keep my thoughts on the mission.*

"Rania told me the surrounding valley hasn't changed much since Cewrick dropped the infant in the river, and the road should be about a day's walk," Ciara said.

Brenn stood up and opened the weapons locker, then handed fleet weapons to Erica, Laro, and Ivran. "You'll be issued your own once you accept your commissions. Judging what we're up against, we need a fleet weapon as well as our swords."

Erica placed the weapon into the holster at her side. That she could handle. The sword was a different story. It reminded her of a broadsword and was much heavier than a rapier, which she was skilled in using.

The hovercraft slowed, then made its descent to land in the valley until it came to a complete stop.

"Dunmore, I'll contact you with coordinates. Stay inside the craft. Okay, team, grab your gear. We need to get started if we want to make it to the road before nightfall," Aldis ordered.

Erica stretched, then grabbed her pack and followed the others out of the hovercraft. The beauty of Ierilia always stunned her—from the myriad of colors in the morning sky as the suns rose, and at night the twinkling of the stars and the four globes of the moons. Ierilia, from what she had seen of it so far, was a kaleidoscope of colors and this valley was no different. Flowers bloomed in abundance amidst the lush grass that reached the banks of the deep blue river. Rainbow colors danced on the surface of the rippling water. The blue was an illusion. The water was actually crystal clear. The colors came from the reflection of the sky and the rocks and sand deep below the water's surface.

"Rania said we should travel northwest to reach the road," Ciara said.

"Ciara and I will take the lead." Brenn hoisted his pack onto his back.

Icaras and Aldis followed, with Erica, Ivran, and Laro taking the rear. The group set a steady pace northwest through the forest.

Erica glanced around at the woods surrounding them. She couldn't believe the size of the trees. The trunks were as wide as a house, and their branches were laden with long, silver needles that swept the ground. Floral vines spiraled around the trunks and branches, filling the silver expanse of the needles with bright spots of blue, purple, and pink flowers. For all the trouble it had caused with her crew, she was glad she had chosen to help defeat Cewrick. By the map Brenn had shown her, the forbidden forest wrapped all the way around the Sucronian Mountains. They were walking right through it, and the changes astounded her. It filled her heart with joy to see how quickly the vegetation had rebounded from the curse.

Breaking through the trees, they entered a veld of flat land that reminded her of pictures of the savannahs in Africa.

They had been walking for several hours before Erica finally had to slow her pace. For every step the men took, she was taking three. It sucked having short legs when you were on a hike with giants. The extra weight of her gear and sword slowed her even further, so she was quickly falling behind. Taking a deep breath, she tried to push her legs to move faster, but the tall grasses of the veld hindered her movements. Luckily for her, Laro showed some mercy and slowed his pace, but Ivran had run ahead to catch up with the rest of the group.

"Erica, are you okay? Do you need any help?" Laro asked.

Erica glanced up at him. He was so tall the top of her head barely came to his shoulders. She really wanted to tell him to take his help and shove it — he had barely said two words to her all day — but one look at the concern in his blue eyes and her anger fizzled away. "Yes, I am okay, and yes, actually, I could use some help. Can we get the giants to slow down just a little bit so the midget can keep up?" She smiled up at him.

Laro laughed and grabbed her hand in his. "Come on, midget, which I presume is an Earth word for a short person, the others aren't too far ahead."

It didn't take them long to reach the group. They were seated on some large rocks near a small pond. A lone tree stood beside it, providing a bit of shade from the heat.

Brenn looked up at them and smiled. "About time you caught up. We will rest and eat lunch here."

Dropping her pack to the ground, Erica breathed a sigh of relief. She had been in stasis on the ship for a couple of years before the crash and was still trying to build her endurance after so much inactivity. The last quest had been hard on her, and they'd had little time to recover from it before setting out on this venture. The heat didn't help any. She sat on one of the rocks and used the base of her shirt to wipe the sheen of perspiration from her face. Laro sat down beside her. He handed her the waterskin. Smiling up at him, she took a long drink and gave it back.

"We aren't far from the road. I think the valley was closer than we estimated. We should reach it within the hour," Aldis said.

Ivran pulled his long blond hair back and tied it at the nape of his neck with a leather lace. "The road is popular among traders. If we are lucky, we may find an inn or stables before we reach Xandero."

"Does that mean we'll be out of this swamp of grass soon?" Erica asked as she plucked a package of dried meat out of her pack. She grabbed a piece and took a bite, savoring the smoky flavor. "This is pretty good. I remember eating it in the caves. What is it?"

"Smoked and then dried kurakelda. They are abundant in caves and tunnels and are a high source of protein. The fleet and Brenn's legions take them along on long journeys," Aldis said.

Erica dropped the piece of meat she had in her hand. "Ugh, you have to be kidding me! The nasty crawlies from the caves?" She yanked the waterskin from Laro and took a drink, then punched him in the arm. "I can't believe you guys hunt these for food. You let me eat those gargantuan fucking spiders?" She looked up at him. It was like a sucker punch straight through her heart. Those deep blue eyes were full of mischief, and he was trying to contain a grin. It wasn't working, because there it was... that dimple she just ached to nip with her teeth. Damn, but the man was sexy as hell.

The ground shifted under Erica's feet. The rock she was sitting on began to tremble, and her pack slid to the ground. Then the whole area began to roll and shift. "A fucking earthquake!"

"Ground shift. Come on! We need to move!" Aldis yelled.

Erica snagged the strap of her pack as Laro pulled her to her feet. They took off running with the others in the general direction of the road they were seeking. Puffs of dirt shot up around them and dust filled the air, obscuring Erica's vision.

A loud crack echoed through the veld. Long, spindly legs

peeked through a wide breach in the ground in front of them. Claws snapped as eight huge creatures pulled themselves from the gorge. Huge mandibles were set on a small head with twelve eyes. Their long, segmented bodies sported two massive claws, eight legs, and a long tail with a pointed stinger.

"What in the hell are these things?" Erica screamed.

"Durogons! They are Zohmes' pets. He had to have sent them from Yanata. They were banished with him," Ciara said.

Erica looked around. A gaping maw right behind them seemed to meet the crack at both ends. They were trapped, with nowhere to run. All hell broke loose. Fire spewed from the durogons' mouths as they advanced on them in a full attack. Icaras threw his hands up and shielded them from the fire with a magical shield. Ciara and Icaras began throwing balls of fire at them, trying to hold the durogons back but of no avail. The durogons' hard bodies seemed impregnable, the fireballs sizzling out before causing any damage to their black, armored shells. Shots from Aldis' fleet weapon met the same fate. Brenn, Ivran and Laro drew their swords, ready to attack.

One of the durogons broke through Icaras' shield and lunged at Erica. She yanked her sword from the scabbard with both hands and nearly dropped it. Laro moved quickly in front of her to shield her and slashed off one of its claws. All it did was piss the creature off. Its tail whipped around and gashed him in the side before Laro could dodge it and slice off the other claw. Erica had never seen Laro wield a sword and was stunned by the beautiful display. He fought the durogon in a deadly dance of precision, each strike of his sword hitting its mark.

A movement caught her attention. Another durogon found an opening and rushed in to attack. Erica pulled out her fleet weapon and started shooting it in the eyes, hoping to keep it from advancing further. Its claws snapped at her, and its tail swished around, trying to find purchase. Suddenly, all she could feel was intense heat, and the scent of charred bodies filled the air. A wall of flame rushed up in front of her, consuming the creature she was trying to kill. Ciara had shifted and set the creatures ablaze.

The rumbling stopped, the ground no longer moved, and the maws slowly closed, burying the creatures.

Erica picked up her backpack and sword, then glanced at Laro. His side was covered in blood, his shirt ripped. She grasped his hand pulling him to where the others had found a spot to rest from the fight. "We need to get that wound cleaned up."

"I'm fine, Erica. It's just a little scratch."

Erica glared at him. "No arguments. There's a lot of blood."

Erica pulled Laro to a large rock near the others, sat down, and took her medical kit from her backpack. Opening it, she took out antiseptic, bandages, and a jar of salve. "Take your shirt off." She watched as he pulled the shirt off over his head. She gasped as the memories of the night before flooded her mind. Laro's gaze locked with hers, a flare of heat in his eyes. Then it quickly faded away. She breathed in deeply as pain stabbed at her heart.

Laro bundled the shirt and wiped the blood from his side. "See? I'm fine. It isn't even bleeding anymore."

Brenn walked up beside Laro to look at his wound. "Are you okay? Do you need healing? I have a vial of Ciara's tears."

Laro shook his head. "You know Ciara can only use so much of her magical tears. Save it for worse. There is no need to heal it. It's a scratch, nothing more."

"Ciara will incinerate your shirt. The blood may attract other predators," Brenn took the shirt from Laro and walked back to Ciara, who rested in dragon form.

Laro scowled, reminding Erica of Tomas. "I will have to

start packing more shirts on these missions. I can't seem to keep from losing them."

Erica smiled, poured some of the antiseptic on a wad of cotton wool, and began cleaning Laro's wound. With the amount of blood that soaked his shirt, she was sure the durogon's stinger had left a puncture wound, but he was right. It wasn't deep, and it wouldn't hinder his movements. After she had removed the blood from his skin, she opened the jar of ointment and began applying it to the gash. She bandaged it. Erica closed her eyes and sucked in her breath. Every time she touched him, she longed to crawl into his arms.

Laro pulled a fresh shirt out of his backpack. "Thank you, Erica."

They gathered their gear and quickly joined the others.

"Zohmes at work. He's desperate to stop us from finding the sister. Let's take this opportunity to finish lunch, rest for a short while, and then we'll continue," Brenn said.

Erica was amazed how fast the time had passed. Digging in her pack to see what other food the cook had packed, she was grateful to find only smoked meats, fresh bread, and fruit in her pack and no more dried, smoked kurakelda. She placed a slab of meat on a chunk of bread, took a bite, and grabbed the offending spider lunch from before. Shoving it at Laro, she told him, "Here. You can have your friggin' spiders!"

CHAPTER SIX

Erica strapped the scabbard and sword back on, grabbed her pack, then stood.

Brenn slung his pack over his shoulder. "If nothing else happens to delay us, we should make it to the road by nightfall and make camp beside it for the night. Ciara knows the spot where Rania left the infant, so she will take the lead."

"It would be so much faster if we could all ride on Ciara. This mission would be over in no time," Erica muttered.

"Good idea, Erica, but not possible. The dragons are native to the Tideless Abyss and our area. Many Ierilians have never seen a jewel dragon, only the black dragons of Cewrick's curse. It could cause major panic," Brenn told her.

"That makes sense. It would frighten me, too." She began to follow, Laro close behind her. They approached another forest. It was different from the forbidden forest, but its beauty matched it. She saw trees resembling a bride's veil, snow white with lacy leaves. Dark and light green trees surrounded them, and some seemed to be almost blue. A carpet of flowers covered the forest floor. She would have loved to take pictures, but her camera's battery had died while she was in the caverns on the mission to save Icaras. She had no idea why she wanted it because as far as she knew, Aldis recorded their missions as halo images. She'd never seen anything that looked like a camera in his hands, so she had no idea how he did it. She walked faster and caught up to Ciara.

"Ciara, this is like a fairy tale. It's beautiful beyond words."

"It is, but look at the damage up ahead. I wonder what happened here." Ciara began to walk faster.

Erica hurried behind her. Suddenly she spotted something in a tree above. "Stop! Look up!"

They stopped, and all looked up at the giant green tree, its leaves long and wide, draping like umbrellas.

"That looks like a piece from our ship," Erica exclaimed.

"This far from where you crashed? Unlikely," Aldis said.

Ciara started to move on. "Let us follow the path of destruction."

They walked cautiously now, looking up, the men venturing into the brush. Now and then they found another large piece of metal on the ground or lodged in a tree. Until they came to a site where the trees were broken or flattened.

Erica stopped. "That's one of our ships! It must have crashed here, too! It's not a cargo ship. I have to see if there are any survivors."

"Erica, stop. It has been a long time since your crash. If there were survivors, they would be out here, wouldn't they?" Laro said, grabbing hold of her arm.

"If they woke up. Let me go." She rushed to a large section that she knew housed the hibernation pods. The door to it was firmly closed. She punched in the code to open it, and to her amazement, it opened. Digging a glimmer stick out of her pack, she lit it and held it up. After punching in the code for the entrance to the hibernation chamber, the door slid open. She held up the glimmer stick and saw that the chamber inside seemed to be intact. So there was still some power. That meant one or more computers were still in working order. Had the people in stasis survived?

A sound behind her startled her. It was Brenn.

"Look, Brenn. Thirty-two pods, just like on my ship."

Brenn held his glimmer stick above one of the pods. "Erica, they're probably dead. This one is."

She quickly joined him and looked through the domed cover at the wizened corpse inside. Its skin was like wrinkled parchment. With a sigh, she went to each pod until she exclaimed, "Here are some that seem to be alive."

"How is that possible?" Brenn asked.

"Different computers."

"Then why didn't they wake up, like you?"

"I don't know. This ship is far more broken up than mine. Maybe part of the mainframe computers still function, and some of it doesn't. Each row of pods is linked to a different computer and controller."

Brenn sighed. "Such an ancient method of travel. We abolished this method centuries ago."

"We're not all as advanced as Ierilia," Erica snapped. "We don't have warp technology on Earth."

"I apologize. We cannot tarry to deal with this. If these people can be woken up, they will be disoriented. It would impact our mission. But I can get word to the new admiral of our fleet. He will send a team to deal with this."

"Brenn, can my crew be part of it? I would suggest Catrice, Rodriguez, and Mark for starters, and Mark can decide who else."

"I will send the coordinates now. It's a good idea for some of your crew to be present if these people can be woken up out of stasis."

Erica watched and listened as he took his communicator out of his pack and contacted the admiral. They left the chamber. Erica locked both doors again. "Some of the crew on this ship might still be alive," she told the group.

"I've contacted the admiral to send a team to deal with this. We need to continue," Brenn said.

Erica was reluctant. On the one hand, she wanted to continue with them, but on the other, she wanted to be there when they tried to take the people out of stasis. Her priorities were mixed. She owed these people so much and felt it her duty to continue on the mission. But she also knew that if there were survivors, they would need a lot of guidance. Who better than someone who had been there a while? *Damn, Erica, get a hold of yourself. Mark and Catrice are capable of dealing with any survivors. Focus on the mission.*

Following the team, her mind was constantly on the crashed ship. Had any other of their ships ended up on Ierilia? If so, where? Her ship was hit by an asteroid, but had it been part of an asteroid belt? It was possible.

"Erica, are you okay?" Laro walked beside her.

"I'm fine."

"It must have been upsetting for you when we found that ship. Did you know any of those people that were on it?"

"Of course I did," she snapped.

"Sorry. I don't mean to offend."

She softened toward him. After all, his concern was almost like balm on a wound. "I didn't mean to snarl at you. Yes, we trained together. Many of us became friends, and we didn't all travel on the same ships. There were thirty-two on each ship. Though I don't remember exactly who was assigned to which ship, I do recall two friends that were stationed on the Initiation Two."

"Is that the name of the ship?" he asked.

"Yes. Ours was the Initiation Five. Not sure if I ever mentioned the name of the ship before."

"And unlike yours, Brenn said many on board this ship didn't make it."

"No. Several computers controlled the hibernation units. Some of the computers malfunctioned, but some appeared to be still controlling a few. Time will tell if any of the others will wake up."

"We're almost there," Brenn called out.

They arrived at the road before sundown, at the spot where Rania said she'd left the infant, and began to set up camp. The road was quiet. There were no travelers on it. In the process of setting up her tent, Erica suddenly noticed how dark it abruptly became. She looked up at the suns and noticed an eclipse happening. "Oh, my God. It's an eclipse!"

"What is an eclipse?" Laro asked.

"When the moon covers the sun. Don't look up at it. You'll damage your eyes. Haven't you ever seen an eclipse?"

"Not that I recall."

The moons covered both suns completely, and it was inky dark. Erica shivered. If they'd never seen an eclipse, why now all of a sudden? Another Zohmes trick? The strange part was, the eclipse lasted a long time. Any she'd seen on Earth lasted no more than an hour or so. This one lasted much longer. The glorious sunset suddenly gone, they sat on the grass. Brenn and Ciara huddled together and waited to see what would happen next. The only light was Brenn's glimmer stick.

Erica moved closer to Laro. If it was a Zohmes trick, something weird could happen at any moment. She glanced around, half expecting monsters to come at them from the forest.

Once the suns lit up the sky again and they breathed a sigh of relief, Aldis said, "I expected some kind of attack."

"So did I," Ivran commented.

Icaras looked a little dazed. "I had a vision during it. This darkness may not have come from Zohmes. It could be that I needed to see clearly without outside distractions."

"What was the vision, Icaras?" Ciara asked.

"I saw a girl. Well... a young woman. I think it was my sister. She was beautiful and looked a lot like me. Her name is Cylena. She has long, black curly hair. Her eyes are gray like mine, and her features are similar to my own. She was gathering herbs. Then she took her basket of herbs and went to an inn. I remember seeing the sign outside the inn. It had a lion painted on it surrounded by a large star."

"Rania has granted you the vision. Did you see the name of the inn?" Ciara asked.

"No. But I can recreate the sign. When I heard a voice say her name, I sensed a very strong connection."

"The name won't help us much because she's invisible," Brenn said.

"No, but the design of the sign on the inn might," Ciara told him.

Erica felt a semblance of relief. Maybe their mission would not be as difficult as it had seemed at first. The angry god scared her. His ability to cause earthquakes, send his pets from hell up to the surface... Lord knew what else the demon could throw into their path.

"How did it feel to see your sister?" Erica asked Icaras.

"It was a wondrous sensation. I experienced a pull as I have never had. I definitely know now what the emptiness in my heart has been, that gaping hole that I could never fill. And no, don't say but you were a worm for centuries. Though I was not in my human body, I still had human thoughts, felt all human emotions, and that missing part was always there."

While they were talking, they had finished setting up camp. It didn't escape Erica's attention that Laro had set up his tent next to hers. With all his bravado and aloofness, did he still feel the same about her?

Brenn and Ivran had built a campfire and roasted meat over it. She quickly took out her own stash and joined them around the fire.

Laro offered her a stick. "Put your meat on it, Erica, and hold it over the flames. It tastes much better roasted over the fire."

They ate and talked, then finally turned in for the night. Erica crawled into her tent. It had been a long day. Her body was tired, but her mind would not let her rest. With her arms under her head, she gazed at the tent dome. The flickering light of the fire sent eerie flames over the sides of the tent. Her thoughts drifted off to the crew of the Initiation Two. Hannah Burkes and Travis McPherson had been part of that crew, two people she'd spent a lot of time with. Were they among the ones that had seemingly survived? Hannah, with her happy smile, long blond hair, a young science officer eager to start a new life in space. And Travis, a farmer who had a flourishing farm on Earth before devastation hit. The government had seized his farm but kept him on to oversee the production of crops. They had often hung out together with some others. Had they made it? Brenn had not given her enough time. The hibernation pods were marked with numbers, not by name. She had no idea if the deceased were Travis or Hannah.

Her thoughts shifted to Laro. A little of his aloofness and cold front seemed to have disappeared. She missed their flirty banter and his heated looks, but she also missed their easy friendship. Tending his wound had tested her restraint. All she could think of was the night before, his touch searing her skin and setting her blood on fire. Had she been too harsh in her rejection of him? Damn, but she wanted him.

Her body completely on fire for him now, she wriggled in her sleeping bag, unable to get to sleep. She suddenly heard a soft moaning. It seemed to come from the direction of Laro's tent. "What the hell?" she muttered, grasping her glimmer stick.

Crawling out of her sleeping bag, she stepped out of the tent and rushed to Laro's. "Laro, are you okay?"

All she got was a grunt. "Laro? What's wrong?" She undid the flap of his tent and quickly crawled inside. Aiming the glimmer stick at him, she saw him thrashing and moaning,

64

perspiration dotting his face and neck.

"Laro?" Crawling up next to him, she pulled the sleeping bag open and looked at his scratch. It was a scratch no longer. She saw a large bulbous swelling that was redder than a tomato. "God, Laro, you're burning up. This isn't good. Let me get Ciara," she muttered.

Hating to bother the newlyweds but having no choice, she left Laro's tent and hastened to theirs. "Ciara, Brenn, wake up," she hissed.

Ciara stuck her head out of the opening. "What's wrong, Erica?"

"It's Laro. He's burning up, and there's a huge swelling on his side where that creature got him."

Ciara was beside her in an instant. They rushed to Laro's tent. Ciara looked at the wound and nodded. "The durogon left its stinger inside. I'll be back in a moment."

Erica waited impatiently. What was probably seconds seemed like an hour before Ciara returned with the vial of her tears. She watched as Ciara carefully dripped several drops onto the small wound. Within seconds, Laro calmed, his fever dissipated, and he slept.

"Thank you, Ciara. Without your tears, what would we do?"

"This was an emergency and the goddess allowed me to use my tears to heal him. Goodnight, Erica. I am sure he is safe in your care." Ciara left the tent.

Erica was so thankful for Ciara's tears. After she watched her leave, she kneeled by Laro, brushing her hand across his forehead to check the temperature of his skin. Leaning down, she lightly kissed his lips. She couldn't help herself. This man, who had crawled under her skin, was more precious to her than she wanted to admit. The amount of blood from his wound had worried her, but the rapid effects from the poison injected by the durogon's stinger frightened the hell out of her. What if she hadn't heard him? Ciara's tears were powerful; they had brought Mark and Laura back from the brink of death. She shouldn't be worried, but there was no way she was leaving him alone. Glancing her hand across his whiskered cheek, she crawled into the sleeping bag and snuggled up to him, determined to watch over him that night.

CHAPTER SEVEN

Erica woke up feeling groggy. It was still dark. The suns had not yet risen. Her night had been restless, constantly waking up to check on Laro, but Ciara's tears had healed him, and he got through the night just fine. She lifted her head to find him wide awake. She gazed into his eyes. He had a confused expression in them.

"Erica? How —"

Erica pressed her hand to his forehead, then checked the wound on his side. Satisfied that his fever was gone and there was no trace of the stinger, she said, "Never mind that. How do you feel?"

"I feel fine. Why are you in my tent?"

"I'm glad you're better. I'll leave you now," she said and began to crawl out of the bag, forgetting that all she was wearing was a thin tank top and her panties. The fact that her panties were nothing but a scrap of material in the front and nothing to hide the cheeks of her ass sent blood rushing to her cheeks. She had been so concerned about Laro, she hadn't thought to dress.

Laro's arm snaked around her waist, pulling her into his lap. He tilted her chin up and gently kissed her lips. Lifting his head, he looked down at her, the passion in his eyes setting her blood on fire. "Erica, why were you in my bed?"

Erica lifted the sleeping bag away from his side. "The

durogon left a stinger inside your wound. You were sick. Ciara had to heal you." She ran her hand along his side, loving the way he felt, soft skin over steel. Trailing her hand across the muscles of his abdomen, she moved to the hard planes of his chest. Erica glanced up at his handsome face—his jaw was clenched, and his pupils dilated with heat.

"Gods, love, you're killing me." Laro groaned as he stilled her hand on his chest. "I can't stop *this*, Erica, no matter how hard I have tried to shut it out. If you don't want whatever *this* is, then please stop touching me. There is only so much I am going to take before I roll you to the ground and claim what is mine."

Erica sucked in a breath as hunger poured through her. Visions of Laro losing control, throwing her to the ground and ravishing her, filled her mind and it thrilled her. A driving need drowned the pain that had filled her the past two days. Her heart pounding, pulse racing, she turned to straddle him. Looking up at him, she wrapped her arms around his neck and whispered, "I don't want to stop *this*." She heard the low growl as he grasped her tank and ripped it off her. Erica gasped as the chill in the air caused her nipples to bead. The heat of his touch seared her skin as he skimmed his fingertip from her jaw, down her neck, to the peak of her breast, then slowly circled the dark pink of her areola.

Erica's body ached. She hungered for the fire of his touch, the taste of his lips. She raised her chin and kissed him. Laro claimed her mouth, taking over, demanding her surrender. She yielded. Deep inside, a piece of her soul only he could touch flared to life. The wall she had fought so desperately to build between them crumbled. Her body trembled as his mouth left hers to trail kisses down her neck, her chest, then nibbled on a nipple. Erica ran her hands down Laro's sides, to his stomach, then to the hard ridge of his cock. He groaned and scraped her nipple with his teeth, sending sparks of need all the way to her core. Shifting her to her back, he blazed a trail of kisses down her chest, then her ribs and finally teased the sensitive skin of her stomach. Her body arched to meet every touch of his lips.

His hands moved down her hips to grasp the straps of her panties. She lifted her hips off the bed as he slid them down her legs and removed them. He gazed down at her, his deep blue eyes lit with passion. "Gods, Erica, the scent of your arousal has teased me for weeks. Open for me, love. Let me taste you."

Dampness pooled between her thighs in reaction to his words. She opened her legs for him. Laro's eyes still locked with hers, he trailed his finger along the inside of her thigh to her slick, velvety folds. Her hips bucked when he slipped a finger inside her, then drew it out to tease her sensitive clit. He withdrew his hand, brought it to his lips, and tasted her arousal.

God, she hungered for him, the ache so deep there was no escaping it. "Laro... please..."

Laro lowered his head and sucked her clit into his mouth, teasing it with his teeth and tongue. He placed his hand between her thighs and inserted first one finger, then two inside her sheath, working her body into a frenzy.

Erica's brain misfired. Her hands fisted in Laro's hair, hips bucking up to meet his thrusting fingers. Sparks of pleasure built within her until they burst into raging flames, the walls of her pussy clenching around his fingers as her body shuddered in release.

Laro slid up her body, his hips cradled between her open thighs, arms on either side of her shoulders. He looked down at her and smiled. That dimple teased her; she wanted to lick it. Erica moved her hands down his back to grab his ass. He was still wearing his pants. How could she have missed that? She placed her fingers under his waistband to try to tug them down.

Laro kissed her lips gently. "We don't have time, love. The suns are rising. I can hear the others moving about." He rolled his body off hers to lay beside her. He wrapped her in his arms and pulled her close against his chest.

Erica turned her head and kissed his nipples, his pecs, her body still aching for him. "I don't have any clothes."

Laro groaned as she nipped his nipple with her teeth. "Behave, woman, I'll get them for you," he said as he shifted off the sleeping bag, stood, and left the tent.

Erica hugged the sleeping bag around her shoulders, the chill of the morning a shock to her heated skin. Catching sight of her torn tank top, she closed her eyes and took a deep breath as need consumed her senses. The raw hunger in his eyes when he'd ripped it off had inflamed her craving for his touch. She only had a couple of tank tops left from the clothing she'd brought from Earth. She'd gladly let him rip them all to shreds just to have him look at her like that again.

The flap opened. Laro tossed her clothes at her. "I hope I got everything. Hurry and dress. The others are breaking up camp already, and Ivran has a fire going for us to cook some breakfast."

Her libido slowly calmed as she hastily dressed, wishing for a bathroom. The bushes would have to do. After she crawled out of the tent, she noticed Laro waiting. Glancing at her own tent, she saw it had already been packed up. "Thanks, Laro."

The team sat on the ground around the fire, roasting the last of their meat and chunks of bread. The aroma was enough to make her stomach growl. "Sorry. I guess I slept too long."

"Mm, slept?" Ivran said, a big grin on his face.

Ciara admonished him. "Enough, Ivran. Teasing them does not help."

"Sorry."

Erica smiled, ignoring the sidelong glance Ivran threw her. She hurried into the shrubbery to relieve herself, then rushed back to the fire and the draw of the scent of roasting meat. Digging in her backpack, she produced her own ration. Ivran handed her a stick so she could roast it.

"What's the plan for today?" she asked, looking at Brenn and Aldis.

"I have asked Icaras to draw us an image on his datapad of the inn's sign he saw in his vision. Here, take a look at it." Brenn handed her the tablet.

Her right hand held the stick with the meat on it, so she took it with her left hand and gazed at it. "A large star with a lion's head in its center. Maybe when we show it to the people in Xandero, they'll recognize it. It's quite unusual."

Laro plopped to the ground next to her. "Your meat is going to burn, Erica."

"Oh!" She quickly yanked the meat away from the fire. Fortunately, it was seared but not blackened.

After they finished eating and drank some of the still-hot coffee from the thermoses rescued from Erica's spacecraft, they doused the fire and began their trek to Xandero.

Travelers began to appear on the road. Brenn stopped to talk to the various farmers and merchants transporting their wares to the other side of the mountains and showed them the drawing. To no avail. None of them had seen an inn with that sign.

They walked until mid-afternoon, when Xandero came into sight.

"Another hour and we'll be there," Aldis said.

Laro hadn't left her side. His presence was comforting. It made her feel safe. He showed no emotion in front of the others, but now and then she caught his gaze on her. This man had really gotten under her skin, and there was no way she could ever scrub him out of her system. *Am I falling in love?*

After the excruciating pain of losing her husband and baby, she'd vowed never to love another man. Was she betraying them by having these feelings? And worse, for an alien man? She shook her head and increased her pace. *Concentrate on the mission, Erica. Control yourself.*

It wasn't all that long before they reached Xandero. The village was a flurry of activity. Children played, merchants hogged the main road, and women hurried to take their shopping home. Erica felt as if she had been transported back into medieval times. It was hard to reconcile Ierilia's advanced technology with it all.

They stopped at the village's stables. "Time to buy horses," Brenn said and led the way.

They bought seven horses, one for each, and two pack horses, along with saddles for each. "Where is your market?" Brenn asked the owner of the stables.

"Just outside the other side of the village."

"Thank you. We will keep our horses here until morning. What time is the market open?"

"Very early. Just after sunup."

"Good. Can you look at this picture and tell me if you recognize it?" Erica watched Brenn show the tablet to him.

"No. Never seen it before. That'll be seventy gold coins, please."

Brenn paid him, and they left for the village inn. It was bustling inside, Erica noticed, as Brenn ordered rooms for them, an evening meal, and breakfast. A lot of men sat at a bar, drinking mead. Others sat at tables, accompanied by women. Some played some sort of game, and some were consuming food.

"We have two rooms, so we'll have to share," Brenn said. "Let's take our packs upstairs before we sit down for the evening meal."

"Two rooms?" Erica asked.

"That's all he has open. It's going to be four in one and three in the other."

Erica sighed. She longed for more alone time with Laro, but that wasn't going to happen tonight. After they got upstairs, Brenn, Ciara, and Icaras were to share one room, and she had to share her room with Ivran, Laro, and Aldis. There was only one bed in the room. How the hell were they going to do that?

"We'll have to use our bedrolls," Laro said. "Erica, you can have the bed."

"I can sleep on the floor. Don't be silly."

"We can argue about it later. Let's go downstairs. I'm hungry." Ivran deposited his bedroll on the floor.

Erica happily agreed. "My stomach has been growling for the last hour," she commented as she walked down the stairs to the dining area of the inn.

Brenn, Ciara, and Icaras were already seated at a table. They joined them, pulling several tables together.

"I've already shown the drawing around, and no one recognizes the sign," Brenn informed them.

"Someone will recognize it," Icaras commented. "If not today, maybe tomorrow. And perhaps in the next village or the one after. Or travelers on the road. Rania didn't show me it for nothing."

Laro had taken a chair next to her. His hand stole under the table and grasped hers. Erica gladly returned his show of affection and squeezed his hand. "We'll find this young woman. Rania won't abandon us. We need to continue on our journey. The inn has to be somewhere far away. It makes sense. Your gods wouldn't want the infant to be found easily, the invisibility proves that."

"You're right," Aldis agreed.

"Food is coming. I hope everyone is hungry," Brenn pointed out.

Though the food so far had been okay when roasted over a

fire, the platters placed on the tables made Erica's mouth water. The aroma was so potent, she was sure if she inhaled enough of it, it would settle her growling stomach. "I've got no idea what it all is, but it smells delicious. As long as it's not kurakeldas."

Her teammates laughed. "Sorry, Erica. Smoked kurakelda is a delicacy for us. We like it," Ivran said.

"Well, you can keep your motherfucking gigantic smoked spiders," she retorted.

"This is smoked varantuas meat. The varantuas are abundant in this area, and the locals hunt them. I don't know how to describe them to you. They are large. Wait. Let me show you." Laro dug in the inside pocket of his tunic.

Erica looked at his datapad showing a picture of the varantuas. "Those are similar to pigs."

"Pigs?"

"An animal on Earth that used to be consumed by many. Ham is one of the products. I think I mentioned ham to you before."

Not scared to dig in, she helped herself to a good portion. The vegetables were roasted as well, and to her surprise, some of them were a yellow color and tasted like potatoes. "What are these called?"

"It's the iveo root," Brenn told her.

"Mm, do you grow those?"

"I believe so. You'll have to talk to my gardeners. Why?"

"I could teach your cook how to make some Earth dishes using these."

Brenn grimaced. "We don't really care too much for the iveo root, but if you can transform them into something tasty, that could be interesting."

"These taste a bit bland. The gravy hasn't got enough spices, but it's a good meal."

After their dinner, they went upstairs to their rooms.

"Erica, you can have the bed," Laro told her.

"I'm not going to hog a bed just for myself. One or two of you can share it with me," she snapped.

Ivran laughed. "Laro, you can share her bed. Aldis and I will happily bed down in our bedrolls. Right, Aldis?"

She gave up. Without undressing, she got into the bed and so did Laro. Restless, she moved up against him. He took her into his arms and rested his head on the top of hers. There was no way they could do anything else, not with the others in the room, but she felt comforted, safe, and so loved as she fell asleep in his arms.

Erica woke to an urgent need to empty her bladder. She shifted in Laro's arms. Damn the beer. She'd consumed a couple glasses of mead with dinner and hadn't thought to ask about a bathroom. There was only one door in the room they'd been given, so she knew there wasn't one there.

She shook his shoulder to wake him. "Laro, where's the toilet," she whispered.

"The what?" he asked groggily.

"You know, the bathroom."

"They don't have bathrooms in this inn, but there is a relieving shack in the back of the inn."

"You have got to be kidding me," she muttered.

"I'll take you," Laro said as he shifted in the bed, stood, and put his boots on.

Erica got out of the bed and grabbed his arm. "Hurry up."

"You really should put your boots on. You could step on something and hurt your feet."

"I'm fine," she said as she pulled him to the door.

Laro grabbed his sword and followed her out of the room. "Come on, love," he said as she followed him downstairs and outside to the rear of the inn.

Erica grimaced as he pointed out a little shed. It really was

75

an outhouse as she knew them from Earth. She wasn't finding this medieval village quite so charming anymore. Stepping inside the outhouse, she pulled her pants down to her ankles and breathed a sigh of relief. Her bladder was about to explode. She heard a scratching sound and warily scanned the walls of the small room. Damn, but she hated creepy crawlies, and Ierilia was full of huge ones, like the kurakeldas.

She screamed as something grabbed the cheek of her ass. She jumped so high, she fell forward, falling face first through the door, her pants still around her ankles. *What the fuck?*

"Erica, what happened?"

Sword in hand, he was ready to fight, and he was peeking in the door, aiming to kill whatever had attacked her.

"Something grabbed my ass," she squeaked.

Laro pulled her up from the ground, pushing her to stand behind him. He held the door open with his sword. She felt his body shaking. Then laughter filled her ears.

"What the hell is so funny!" she exclaimed as she punched him in the chest.

"It's just a little mouri." He continued to laugh.

Erica turned her head to see a tiny rodent about the size of a mouse. It had bluish fur, eight legs, and a long, skinny tail. It was kind of cute. Looking back up at him, she sucked in a quick breath. That damn dimple again. "It's not funny."

Laro dipped his head and kissed her quickly on the lips. "Pull your pants up, love."

Erica growled, yanked her pants up, and started giggling. "Okay, I cede. I guess it was pretty funny. Don't you dare tell anyone! Let's go back to bed."

CHAPTER EIGHT

Erica woke to the sound of a door softly clicking shut, then a light caress along her jaw.

"Morning, sleepyhead," Laro said.

Opening her eyes, she gazed up at him. His hair was damp, and a clean scent reminding her of sandalwood and leather teased her. "Morning," she grumbled sleepily.

"Breakfast will be ready soon. There is a pitcher of fresh water and soap for you at the wash basin. I didn't think you wanted to wash at the pump after last night," he said, grinning. "It's also not very private. The others have already gone downstairs for breakfast, so we need to hurry."

She sat up on the side of the bed noticing he was fully dressed, her feet hitting the floor. The wooden floor was cold. She shivered. She was dying for a hot bath, but the wash basin would have to do. "Thank you."

Laro slipped his arms around her waist, pulling her into his arms. She sighed and rested her head against his chest, enjoying the warmth of his embrace. Stepping back, he released her, then gently kissed her lips. "I'll meet you downstairs with the others," he said, reaching for his gear.

Erica grabbed the top of his pants, pulling him closer to her. "Not yet." She slipped her fingers beneath the tight waistband of his pants.

Laro grabbed her hand, stilling it. "Erica," he growled.

She caught his heated gaze, raised up on her toes and whispered against his lips, "Let me, please? We have time for this." Pushing him up against the wall, she loosened the leather laces of his pants, freeing the hard length of him. Damn, she ached. All she wanted to do was wrap her legs around his waist and ride him to oblivion. But this wasn't about her.

Erica slid down his body to kneel in front of him. Wrapping her hand around the base of his cock, she took him into her mouth, taking him in all the way to the back of her throat. One hand teased his taut sack, the other sliding the length of him with the movements of her mouth. Erica glanced up as a growl escaped him. His head rested against the wall. His eyes were closed, his teeth worrying that sexy bottom lip.

"Gods, woman." Laro groaned, his hands sliding through her hair to grasp the back of her head, his hips thrusting with her movements. Slipping her lips further down his length, she worked the base of his cock with her hand. She moaned as she felt his body stiffen and he growled her name in release.

Laro pulled her up against his chest and kissed her softly on the lips. Gazing up at him, she smiled. "Now we really don't have time," she said as she laced the front of his pants.

He cupped her chin, kissing her one more time. "I'll meet you downstairs before they send out a search party." He traced his finger down her cheek to her bottom lip. Then he picked up his gear and left to join the others.

Erica walked to the basin, poured some water into it from the pitcher, and quickly washed. The water cooled her heated skin. Five minutes alone and Laro had her hormones on overdrive. Taking a deep breath to slow her racing pulse, she finished washing. After she'd grabbed her gear, she opened the door to head downstairs.

"Good morning, Erica."

Ciara walked toward her. Her waist length black hair was

in a long braid that draped over her shoulder.

Erica shut the door, relieved that she wasn't the only one lagging behind. She waited for Ciara to join her. "Are Brenn and Icaras already downstairs?" she asked as they continued to walk toward the stairs.

Ciara nodded. "They were up much earlier. Brenn received a message from the fleet. A rescue and salvage team has located the crashed ship. They will update him with details on survivors as soon as they search the wreckage."

As they reached the bottom of the stairs, Erica scanned the dining room. The men sat at a table in the corner of the room. Servers were busy placing platters of food on the table. Reaching the table, Erica sat down by Laro. Needing to touch him, she placed her hand in his. He squeezed her hand and looked down at her. She noticed a worried expression on his face.

Brenn's gaze met hers. "Erica, the rescue team found seven survivors on board the crashed ship. They are being transferred to the hospital in Cront. Mark and Laura are with them, along with your ship's doctor and two of your nurses."

Erica's heart sank. Out of thirty-two crew members on the Initiation Two, to have only seven survive the crash was a serious blow. The possibility of Travis or Hannah's survival was slim. "Thank you, Brenn. Please keep me updated on them."

Feeling the burn of tears filling her eyes, she quickly wiped them away. She couldn't let her feelings get in the way of their mission.

"I'm sorry, love," Laro whispered as he gently caressed her leg.

They quickly finished breakfast, grabbed their gear, and headed to the market to replenish their supplies.

Erica sighed in frustration as Brenn continued to show the symbol of the inn to traders and villagers but to no avail. The people at the market were just as clueless to the inn's whereabouts as the people they had encountered the night before. They were getting nowhere and the morning was waning fast.

"Let's get our horses and continue to the next town," Brenn said.

"Needles and haystacks," Erica muttered under her breath.

As they approached the stables, Erica saw their horses already saddled and ready for them. Ivran and Aldis loaded their gear onto the pack horses as Brenn spoke to the stable owner.

Erica smiled as Laro stuffed a couple of new shirts into his saddle bag, then walked to her, that familiar heat in his gaze.

"I'll help you mount, midget. I doubt you'll be able to reach the stirrup on your own. I like that Earth word." He grinned at her.

Sexy, sexy, man. Damn, she was smitten. How in the hell had he wormed his way into her heart so fast? *Not my fault I got stranded on a planet populated by hotter-than-hell giants.*

Laro helped her mount, then mounted his own horse. He rode beside her as they headed out of the village. The group rode in silence, stopping to inquire about the inn's symbol as they encountered other merchants and travelers.

Erica focused her attention on their surroundings, frustrated that the goddess had shown Icaras a symbol of an inn that no one recognized.

Looking up at the suns, Erica noticed it had to be near lunchtime. Suddenly, the sound of thundering hooves echoed around them as a herd of harteox broke through the trees. Their horses startled, reared, and whinnied in surprise, throwing her to the ground. The breath slammed from her lungs as she hit the hard, packed dirt. She groaned in pain as she struggled to sit up.

"Erica!" Laro yelled. Jumping off his horse, he rushed to

her side to help her sit up. "Are you hurt?"

Erica grimaced as her vision spun, then cleared. "I'm okay."

"Morcougs!" she heard someone shout.

Erica looked up to see six of the monstrous creatures Ciara had killed at her ship's crash site. The sound of their horses had drawn the morcougs away from the herd of harteox and straight to them. Icaras tried to deflect the monsters' attack with magick. He began to chant a spell but wasn't quick enough. One of the morcougs slammed him in the chest, sending him flying through the trees.

Taking a deep breath, Erica got to her feet and grabbed her fleet weapon.

Laro pushed her hand down as she was taking aim to fire at one of the creatures. "No! The weapons won't work. You'll just anger them. There is only one spot where they can be killed. Their throats."

Brenn and Ivran dismounted their horses and shifted into their lions. Erica looked up at Laro and gasped as he shifted, too.

Damn, but he was breathtaking. All muscular, feline body and a magnificent mane. Lord, he was huge. She gazed at the three magnificent lions. They were much bigger than Tomas when he had accidentally shifted. He nudged her toward the trees with a growl. She shook her head. There was no way she was leaving them to fight these monsters alone.

Aldis grabbed her arm, pulling her toward the trees where Icaras had landed. "Run, Erica! Let them handle it. They can't concentrate on killing the morcougs if we are in the way."

Once they reached Icaras, he placed a shield of magick around them. "This should keep them from sensing us."

Erica pointed to the lions fighting two of the morcougs. "What about them. They'll be killed!"

"No, Erica. Just watch," Icaras told her.

Flames burst through the trees across from them as Ciara, in dragon form, set fire to one of the morcougs, lifted off, and circled around in the sky, targeting another and incinerating it.

To Erica's amazement Brenn, Ivran, and Laro were holding their own. One of the lions rushed the first morcoug and jumped high enough to wrap its jaws around its throat, ripping out its trachea. The impact of the creature's body shook the ground as it collapsed in death. The second morcoug met the same fate seconds after the first. The last morcoug burst through the trees, its body in flames. It landed on top of one of the creatures killed by the lions. Ciara swooped down, incinerating what was left of the morcougs to ashes.

All was quiet again except for the distant sound of the harteox's hooves as they fled. Erica heaved a sigh of relief. The only evidence left of the attack were small piles of ashes on the road. She let out her breath that she'd unconsciously held as Laro's lion had fought with one of the beasts. When the lion had jumped out of reach of the morcoug's claws, Ciara had stepped in.

The men shifted back to their humans. Erica stepped forward to run to Laro but ran into a wall. "Let me out of this fucking cage," she shouted at Icaras.

Icaras chuckled and waved his hand. The invisible shield disappeared, and Erica rushed to Laro.

"Laro, are you okay? Did you get hurt?" she asked while looking at him from head to toe, front and back.

"I'm fine, love. The only pain involved was the first time changing into my lion and back. By the gods, it hurts."

"I'm with you there," Ivran said, rubbing his arms and legs.

"Only the first few times. My change was smooth this time." Brenn picked up his fallen sword.

Aldis sighed. "Why was I born without any magical abilities?"

"Tell me about it," Erica agreed. "I could use some magic or shifting talent."

They ran into the forest to find the horses. The frightened animals had hidden among a clump of trees and stood huddled together. Erica spoke softly to her horse, patting his nose and calming him.

They led the horses back to the road, mounted, and resumed their journey. Erica took a drink from her waterskin and called out to Aldis and Brenn in front. "How far is the next village?"

Aldis looked back at her. "It's called Orpeku. It's a town, larger than the village we just visited. Their technology is more advanced, and its population is at least ten times as big."

"Great. You mean we actually get a room with maybe a bathroom that has running water and a toilet?" Erica couldn't help uttering.

Brenn laughed. "We could be luckier there in finding someone that recognizes the inn's symbol. We should stop soon to eat, but we can't tarry too long. We want to get to Orpeku by nightfall."

Several horse-drawn, canvas-covered wagons approached from the opposite direction. When they were level with the first wagon, Brenn stopped to speak to the merchant. He showed him the drawing, and Erica saw the man shake his head. She had the eerie feeling that she had traveled back in time and found herself in the old pioneer days in America. If it weren't for the two suns up above and the foreign vegetation, she'd almost start doubting her sanity.

Brenn showed the image to each of the five drivers of the wagons. No luck.

They continued riding until they approached a small clearing next to the road. "We'll stop here for lunch," Aldis called out and led his horse to tie him to a tree.

They rested just long enough to have a quick bite and drink their water. Erica mounted and spurred her horse on to ride beside Brenn and Aldis. "Except for the earthquake and the morcougs, it has been unnaturally quiet. And those beasts are not Zohmes' doing. Maybe that crazy god will leave us alone now for the remainder of this mission? Surely he must be running out of ways to pester us."

CHAPTER NINE

I t was well before nightfall when they reached the outskirts of Orpeku. Large farmhouses stood scattered in the vast fields surrounding the town. The town itself had streets laid with stones, and the houses were more like the ones in Cront.

They had barely entered the town when a strong wind blasted them. Large black clouds drifted above, covering the suns. "A storm?" she asked, looking at Laro.

"Looks like it. We need to find shelter, fast."

Brenn and Aldis had already spurred their horses into a gallop. Their hooves clattered loudly on the pavers. People hurried along sidewalks, looking for shelter from the threatening rain, barely glancing at the group of strangers entering their village.

Lightning lit up the black sky, followed by deafening thunder. "I've never heard such loud fucking thunder," Erica muttered.

Before they could reach the inn, huge hailstones began to rain down on them. "Find shelter!" Aldis and Brenn shouted. "Anywhere!"

"That's not fucking hail. Those are almost soccer balls!" Erica yelled as she pulled on the reins and steered her horse off the road toward a house with an overhang over the door.

A white sheet of hailstones covered the street in seconds.

"We're fortunate this didn't happen earlier," Aldis said while trying to calm his horse.

Icaras nodded. "This is Zohmes. This could have hurt our horses badly and us. I hope no people are injured. Ciara? We can stop this."

Ciara joined Icaras. Holding hands, they closed their eyes and chanted a spell. In mere seconds, the hail stopped, the black clouds disappeared, and the suns quickly melted the ice on the road. Steam rose from the forming puddles.

Erica led her horse back onto the street and looked at the long road leading away from the town. The hail stopped just at its border. "You're right. The hail targeted just us. Look down the road and up ahead. The rest of the street has no ice on it, neither does the road we've traveled."

When they reached the inn, Brenn dismounted quickly and went inside to book rooms and to inquire about the stables.

He came back fast. "The inn is busy, but I managed to get three rooms this time. One for Ciara and me, Laro and Erica in one, and Aldis, Icaras, and Ivran can share. The inn has its own stable at the back. The innkeeper gave me a key to the gate just down there." He pointed to a large metal gate beside the building.

"Laro and I will take the horses to the stable. We'll join you inside shortly," Ivran offered.

Erica took her gear off the packhorse and followed Brenn and Ciara into the inn. She was pleasantly surprised at the modern interior. Well, modern for Ierilian standards. Compared to the inn in the last village, this was a five-star hotel.

A young woman led them up the stairs to their rooms. When Erica stepped inside, she heaved a sigh of relief. "A bathroom." She dropped her pack and headed for it right away. To her delight, there was a toilet, a sink, and a bath. Well, a toilet Ierilian style, but hey, they beat the toilets on

Earth. That's if the toilet worked the same as the ones in Brenn's house. A round bowl that sucked the urine and feces down immediately. No toilet paper. She'd found it odd at first and wondered how she was going to wipe, until she'd used the toilet for the first time. "Well, dammit, it's some kind of bidet," she'd uttered as a strong stream of water had cleansed her, followed by hot air.

She'd already filled the bath and stood naked, ready to get into it, when Laro came in. Heat rose to her face as his gaze devoured her from head to toe. She quickly wrapped a towel around her body.

He cleared his throat. "Eh, we are meeting the others downstairs for dinner."

"Oh. I so wanted to relax in a hot bath," she muttered.

In two strides, he was inside the bathroom and took her into his arms, the towel falling to the floor. "Erica, my love, you have no idea what you do to me," he whispered against her neck.

His hands cupped her buttocks. He rained kisses from her neck to her ear to her forehead, his lips trailing down her nose and finally claiming her mouth. Her heart pounded so hard she thought he could hear it. Flutters began in her chest, crept down to her stomach, and settled in her loins. Her pussy throbbed. Oh, she wanted this man.

Abruptly, he let go of her. "Bathe quickly. They are waiting for us."

"Damn, that was colder than those fucking hailstones," she exclaimed.

"Cold?"

"Never mind. You just doused a fire." She thought she heard him chuckle as he walked away and sighed. It would have been fantastic if he would have joined her in the bath. She washed quickly, but the fire he'd ignited still caused havoc within her, played games with her clit and her throbbing, needy vagina. Vigorously, she rubbed between her legs and tried to control her need.

"Are you almost finished? Aldis just knocked on the door. Food is waiting for us," Laro called out.

After she dried herself off, she dressed hastily. They hurried downstairs to find the others sitting at the bar. The restaurant area of the inn was filled, all tables taken by merchants and travelers.

Waitresses flitted about serving food, wine, and mead. The innkeeper and what she would call a bartender stood behind the bar. Two empty stools waited for them, their platters of food already on the bar along with a tall mug of mead for Laro and a glass of wine for her.

Erica hadn't realized how hungry she was until she started to eat. The food reminded her of stew, although this stew had meat in it, unlike the fake stew she knew on Earth. They had almost finished their meal when Brenn produced his datapad. The innkeeper and the bartender stood quietly for a few minutes, so it was a good opportunity to show it to them.

"Do you know of an inn that has this sign hanging outside their door?" she heard him ask.

The innkeeper shook his head, but then the bartender, glancing over the innkeeper's shoulder, suddenly nodded.

"That looks like the inn in Zugut."

"How far away is it?" Icaras asked.

"Zugut is the next village, a full day's ride. I recall it because the innkeeper and his wife tell these great stories about a family with a make-believe child. Their tales are quite funny. That's why I remember the inn so well."

"Thank you. Do you know the name of the inn?" Brenn queried.

"It's called The Growling Lion. Sorry, I have to serve," he said.

"Looks like we're finally getting somewhere." Erica

scraped the last spoon full of her stew off her plate.

"Yes. Some people are leaving. Let's get a table," Laro suggested.

Erica sighed. After the teasing before her bath, all she wanted to do right then was get him to their room.

Brenn ordered a pitcher of mead and more wine for Erica and Ciara. They found a large table at the back of the inn and started seating themselves.

Laro snaked an arm around Erica's waist and pulled her into his lap. She grinned at him, then leaned back to rest against his chest.

Ivran shook his head at them, laughing. "The two of you are getting as bad as Brenn and Ciara."

"You are one to talk, Ivran. You have been mated to Reana for over thirty years, and you are still completely besotted," Brenn said.

"There's no way. He looks like he's in his twenties," Erica said, surprise in her voice.

"Ivran is one hundred and twenty-nine, love. So is Brenn. Their mothers birthed them only weeks apart," Laro said.

Erica turned in his lap, catching his gaze. "But if they are... and you look," she stuttered, then turned to look back at the others.

"I'm one hundred and sixty-two, love," he whispered in her ear.

"But... I am thirty-two, and we look close in age. On Earth, we are considered lucky if we live past ninety, and then we're old, parched, wrinkled." Erica could hardly believe what she'd just heard.

"You haven't told her?" Ciara asked.

"Told me what?" Erica asked as she turned back to Laro. He looked upset.

"I was waiting for a better time, Ciara. She doesn't even know what a lifemate is yet. How could she?" Laro said.

"Icaras told us that when you are born, your soul is tied to another. Is that what you're talking about?" Erica asked.

Laro trailed his fingers along her jaw, took a deep breath, then clenched his hand and dropped it to his side. "It is so much more than that, Erica. A lifemate is a gift bestowed upon us by the gods. Most live their lives never finding their lifemate, the one whose soul is entwined with theirs. It is the one bond that once sealed, can never be broken. But it does have to be accepted by both."

Erica gasped as she caught his gaze. "So, what you are telling me is that I'm your lifemate."

Laro stood up and set Erica to her feet. "Yes, you are." He kissed her quickly, then turned to his friends. "We will see you in the morning. Erica and I have a lot to talk about."

Dazed, Erica allowed Laro to guide her to their room. He opened the door and sat her on the bed. "I'm going to take a quick bath."

Her brain kickstarted. She grabbed him by the shirt and pulled him back to her. "Wait. I'm going to grow old and die, and you are going to stay young, for what, centuries?"

Laro gazed down at her, his jaw clenched, his eyes filled with concern. He pulled her into his arms and held her close. "Only if you reject the bond, love."

What does that mean? The beliefs on this planet confused the hell out of her. She pushed at his chest. "Go, have a bath so we can talk."

She sat on the bed, her mind a whirlwind of thought until she shoved it all into a far corner of her brain. The sight of him pulling his shirt off on the way to the bathroom, all that lean muscle and tawny skin, set her blood on fire. Damn if she was going to wait until after they talked. Her body was aching for him. Stripping off her clothes, she hurried to the bathroom and saw him relaxing, his eyes closed. He hadn't heard her come in. She stepped into the bath between his legs.

Laro startled and sat up, splashing water over the sides. "Erica, what are you —"

She sank down into the water and lay against him, her hands on either side of his face. "Hush. This cat-and-mouse play has gone on long enough. From the night you brought me the scabbard, you distanced yourself. I understand why you did, but what I said was wrong. I want you, Laro. I need you." Before he had a chance to say anything, she kissed him, long and hard, her tongue exploring every crevice of his mouth. His cock was hard and pulsating against her pussy as she straddled him. Wiggling her hips, she teased him, rubbing up and down against his erection. He groaned and grasped her hips.

With her lips still claiming his mouth, she lifted her hips slightly and allowed the tip of his cock to tease her entrance. Slowly, she began to push down, until he suddenly forced her away from him.

"Erica, we need to —"

"Later, baby, later. Right now, I ache for you to fill me, to satisfy my yearning, my hunger for you. If you don't, I'll become impossible to be with," she murmured against his lips. She felt him relax, his hands moving to her breasts. A gasp escaped her lips as he tweaked her nipples and massaged her firm breasts.

"Your breasts are so beautiful and firm. I can't believe you've suckled an infant. I've heard many a woman complain after suckling that their breasts became limp," he said softly.

That doused her fire for a moment. The thought of her baby and the milk she couldn't give her invading her mind. Their malnourishment was the cause of her inability to nurse her babe. But it was only for an instant. Her body was on fire. Her need for them both to be fulfilled greater than her memories.

She leaned forward and pushed a nipple into his mouth. "Suck, baby, suck hard," she hissed and began to push down

91

with her hips. The feel of his mouth sent shock waves to her core.

There was only a moment of hesitation until he lifted his hips, slowly pushing into her. She slammed her hips down, taking him fully. It hurt. She hadn't had sex for so long, her vaginal muscles had tightened. It was almost as if she were still a virgin having sex for the first time.

He grasped her hips and stilled her. "Gods, love, you are tighter than a warrior's glove. Keep still. I don't want to hurt you."

Releasing her hips, he tilted her chin and captured her lips. His kisses consumed her, first her mouth in a devouring kiss, then down to her neck and shoulder, teasing and tasting until he bit her between the neck and shoulder. God, she was hungry for him, the tight feeling of fullness now an ache to be satisfied. He began to move inside her. Slowly at first, sliding a hand down between them and teasing her clit with his thumb. Faster, she matched his moves, stroke for stroke. Flinging her head back, she yelled, "Yes, Laro, harder... harder... yes... oh, God, I'm going to come."

He squeezed her breasts hard. Her body trembling, she claimed his lips again. He spasmed beneath her. She felt his release as her core tightened around his cock.

Breathing heavy, she pulled her lips away from his and just lay atop him. "Laro, I think I'm falling in love with you," she whispered near his ear.

His breathing calmed. "Erica, I *am* in love you." He kissed the top of her head. "I think from the moment I saw you when we approached your crashed ship, I knew we were meant for each other. Now, let's finish bathing and then we need to talk."

Their desire sated for the time being, they washed each other, splashed, and laughed. After they got out of the bath, they ran to the bed and fell onto it in an embrace.

Laro finally disengaged his arms from her and sat up. "Would you like a glass of wine? I brought some upstairs with me," he said.

Erica sipped from the glass of wine he handed her and sat up against the pillows. "Okay, let's talk, but let me go first."

"All right. What would you like to say?"

"Please, don't ever mention my baby again while we're having sex."

"I'm sorry, love. I realized after I had said it, that it was wrong."

"There is still too much pain in my heart at her loss. I never had the chance to suckle her. Because of malnutrition, the food deprivation we suffered, I had no milk. You've got no idea how it hurt me that I couldn't suckle my baby."

Laro set his glass on a nightstand and placed his arm around her. He held her for a moment. "I'm so sorry, my love."

"You couldn't have known. Now, what did you want to talk to me about?"

"From our conversation earlier tonight, you realize you are my lifemate?"

"Sort of. Why would your gods choose an Earth woman for your lifemate? And I'm sorry to ask this because I know losing my family hurt, but wasn't Tomas' mother your lifemate?"

"I loved Khrissa. She and I were mates, not lifemates. Finding a lifemate is rare. Most never find one in their lifetime."

Erica could hear the softness in his voice when he said Khrissa's name. She shifted in his arms, gazing up at him. "Will you tell me about her?"

He smiled, warmth in his expression. "Tomas reminds me so much of Khrissa. He has her caring nature and obstinate will." He sighed, caressing her shoulder. "We grew up together, our friendship as children blooming to love as adults. I knew she was dying, the whole village knew. The only family member I had that accepted our mating was Kira. Khrissa was born with a blood-borne illness that was slowly killing her. She wasn't supposed to have children, but the stubborn woman had her implant removed without telling me. She wanted a child so badly. The pregnancy was more than her body could take. She died giving birth to Tomas."

"On a planet with so much magic, couldn't she have been saved? I've seen Ciara's tears heal you instantly. Couldn't they have saved her? Or couldn't your gods intervene?"

Laro tilted her chin up and kissed her gently on the lips. "The gods did intervene. They gave me Tomas, healthy and whole. He could have died with Khrissa, but miraculously, he survived. He did not inherit the blood-borne illness. As for the healing tears, you know Ciara was trapped in the Clyss until Brenn freed her, so she wasn't around when Tomas was born. Also, Ciara must gain permission from the gods to use her tears. In the case of life and death, she can only use them to save a life that was not supposed to be taken."

Erica settled back against him, trailing her hand across his chest. "If that's the case, how will it work for us? You're going to live on for centuries as a lion shifter, and I'll just die a normal Earth age."

"If and when we unite at the Clyss, and that's only if you accept me as your lifemate, our souls will join. We will be blessed by the gods and the goddesses. You will live a long time."

Erica was quiet for a moment, trying to absorb it all. Then she said, "So, I'll become a shifter, too?"

"No. But, because our souls are joined, you will receive a shard of my soul, and that will allow you to live a long time."

"I'm still fertile, you know. Will our children, if you want more of course, be lion shifters?" she wondered.

"My love, only time will tell. There has never been a union

94

between one of us with someone from another planet. Brenn's and Ciara's union was unusual enough. Only the gods and goddesses know if they'll have children and whether they'll be shifters, dragons or lions."

Erica giggled. "Maybe a mix of both?"

Laro joined in her mirth. "That would be interesting." He gently caressed her arm. "Erica, I love you. I know I've given you much to think about. I don't want an answer from you now. After this mission is over, we will speak of it again. For now, we need to rest. We leave at sunup."

Erica sighed and kissed him goodnight. With his arms still around her, hugging her tight against his body, she couldn't go to sleep right away. She really did have a lot to think about. How was a happy marriage between them going to work anyway? Laro had joined Brenn's legions, and so had she. They'd be away from each other more than together. Then again, there was no war anywhere on Ierilia right now, so they would be home-based. And what if she did get pregnant? She could hardly be involved in any missions and would have to sit at home and wait for him if he had to go away. Still thinking about it all, worrying about all the problems, she drifted off.

CHAPTER TEN

With a start, she woke up to see the gorgeous pastel colors of sunrise coloring the sky. Reaching out, she found an empty spot where Laro should be, and the bedding was cold. He was already up and probably downstairs. "Damn. Why didn't he wake me up?" she muttered while swinging her legs out of bed and headed for the bathroom.

After washing herself and dressing, she hurried down the stairs to find everyone already seated at a long table.

"There you are," Laro said, sending her a big grin.

"Why didn't you wake me?" she snapped, instantly regretting her tone of voice.

"You were sleeping so peacefully. I would have come upstairs shortly to wake you."

"Thanks, but in the future, please wake me? I don't like being the last one to arrive at breakfast."

Taking the empty chair next to him, she quickly placed a kiss on his cheek. "Sorry," she whispered.

The waiter set platters of food on the table. To her relief, it was very similar to what Brenn's cook dished up for them. The smoked kurakeldas still scared the shit out of her. They ate, drank their jago milk, and when they were all done, Brenn said, "If everyone is finished, I suggest we leave right away for Zugut."

Laro helped Erica with her gear, stowing it on the packhorse for her, then offered to help her get on her horse.

"Dammit, Laro. Just because we had sex doesn't mean I've become a helpless, needy female," she hissed at him.

Ivran and Aldis had heard, and both burst out laughing.

"Oh, so you two mated last night," Ivran commented, then grinned.

Aldis added, "We know what sex means. You explained it to us, Erica."

She was sure her face was redder than the sky. Oh, had she ever given away that she and Laro had mated, as they called it. A retort was on her lips, but she clamped them together firmly as Brenn began to lead the way out of the stables.

On the way out of the town, they stopped at the local market to pick up supplies for their lunch. Erica wondered what that day would bring. They'd experienced another earthquake with giant creatures, morcougs, a hailstorm that could have killed them—what did Zohmes plan next? It seemed the angry god was determined they would not find the sister. But if the sister was such a secret, how did he know about her? *Cewrick told him about the second baby,* a little voice in her mind said. Right. But Cewrick didn't know that Rania had rescued the infant, that she was still alive. Maybe Zohmes suspected they were on the path to fulfilling Icaras' full potential and that was why he was trying to stop them.

As she followed, all kinds of thoughts came to her mind. Angry gods... she'd seen the movie *The Ten Commandments*, and God's vengeance against the Romans. At least, that's what the movie depicted. Zohmes was kind of similar, except he was a fallen god, like Lucifer was God's favorite angel before God banished him from Heaven. It was kind of strange that this world had gods and goddesses, a number of them, yet she'd grown up knowing of only one God. It had to be different for various universes. Maybe these gods and goddesses were related to the God she'd learned about in Sunday school, church, and stopped praying to when Earth went to hell. Her God seemed as if He didn't care anymore. Maybe these gods were different. Rania was sweet, loving, protecting, and from what she'd learned, Zohmes was the only infected apple in the basket.

The closer they came to Zugut, the colder it got. She began to see patches of snow on the ground. Brenn had told her they were heading into winter. On Earth, they'd probably be getting close to Christmas now. For a moment, nostalgia overtook her thoughts. This planet was so different. There would be no Christmas. She didn't even know what month of the year it was except it would be winter very soon. *But why can't we have a Christmas and carry on our own traditions?* The thought played in her mind.

"Time to stop for lunch. We're making good time," Brenn called out and halted his horse. He dismounted and led the horse off the road to an outcropping of trees where the snow was scarce.

Laro walked up to her after tying his horse to a tree. "Are you cold, love?"

"Yes. But I have a jacket in my pack."

"I'll get it for you."

He was so sweet. He had all the qualities that Rory had not possessed. Sure, she'd loved her husband, but like all married couples they'd had arguments, and there had been many things about Rory that she didn't like. Had she ever been truly in love with him? What she felt for Laro was so intense, so different, she couldn't compare it.

"Here you are. Put it on. Your lips are turning blue."

"Oh, that's a compliment?"

He chuckled. "You are beautiful, no matter what color your lips are."

Brenn and Ciara had set a fire going. Ivran had found sticks for all of them so they could roast their meat and bread over the fire.

Erica laced her meat onto her stick and was about to move closer to the fire when she noticed the scenery around them had changed. The road was no longer going straight south. It turned southwest and disappeared into the trees. "What in the fuck happened to the road?"

"It has to be Zohmes!" Ciara exclaimed.

"I figured that! But how are we going to find the town? The road is going the wrong way," Erica said.

"Can you and Icaras change it back?" Brenn asked.

"No, we can't. We are strong enough to stop some things, but we cannot change the planet in this way. We can go back a couple of hours and draw a map." Icaras said.

"What in the hell do you mean? You can time travel?" Erica asked.

"In a way," Ciara said as she joined hands with Icaras, both chanting softly, working their magick. Flashes of light danced around them, slowly building, then a sudden flash.

They were gone.

The whole thing reminded Erica of a book she'd read on time travel. It never boded well for the people that chose to jump to the past or the future. "Brenn, will they be safe? Can they get back?"

"I'm not comfortable when she endangers herself, but I trust her. I know she will come back," Brenn said.

"You're sure—"

Brenn's communicator interrupted Erica. "General, I have updates on the survivors of the crashed ship you found. You requested a list of names. I just received the transmission."

Erica looked at Brenn. "Please, I need to know."

Laro slipped behind Erica and snaked his arms around her waist, pulling her against his chest.

How does he always know when I need him?

"Go ahead, Captain Arren," Brenn answered.

"Travis McPherson, Gwen Anderson, Talia Garret, and Samuel Thorn are awake and off life support. Greyson Conner and Olivia Riley are unconscious but in stable condition. Aria James is still in critical condition."

"Thank you, Captain. I will inform Captain Martinez of their condition." Brenn closed the communicator.

Erica felt as if she had been sucker punched. "Hannah didn't make it." Her eyes filled with tears. She turned in Laro's arms and rested her head on his chest and cried.

"I'm so sorry, love," he whispered, holding her tightly.

She glanced up at him, at the man who had steadily wormed his way into her heart. For once she didn't mind at all that she appeared weak. She stood on her toes and kissed his lips. "Thank you."

Picturing Hannah in her mind, she felt overwhelmed with grief. She and Hannah had often hung out together. The young woman, with her mop of red-gold curls, mischievous brown eyes, a tom-boy, yet all woman, had been a lot of fun to party with. Hannah and Travis had become very close, so much that Erica thought they would end up as a couple once they reached their destination. Travis had to be devastated. She wished she was there to comfort the survivors. Pulling herself together, squashing the sadness, she paid attention to what was going on around her.

"We have the map!" Ciara reappeared, and so did Icaras.

"Great. Show me," Aldis said.

Erica watched Aldis study the map.

He finally looked at them and said, "Zohmes tried to throw us off course completely. Why? Any ideas, Icaras? Ciara?"

"Icaras' magick will increase when he and his sister bond to such an extent that they will be much stronger than Zohmes. At least, that's what I think. I'm not totally sure,"

Ciara said.

"Zohmes is afraid of the bond between my sister and I. Fear of us overpowering him is what drives him to try and stop us from finding my sister. I don't think we can, but I could be wrong. Rania hasn't spoken to me about it yet," Icaras told them.

"How does Zohmes know your sister is alive?" Erica closed the straps of her pack.

"Cewrick's spies are still among us. I have shown my amulet to various travelers and people in the villages and asked them if they knew of a young woman with the same amulet. One of them or more could be Cewrick's minions," Icaras suggested.

"Zohmes is powerful. He, too, has spies and can even send a bird to listen to our conversations. He knows Icaras is still missing a vital part to come into his powers, and therefore he tries to stop this quest." Ciara looked at the map again.

"Well, now we at least know the correct coordinates. It looks as if we'll have to travel through that forest up ahead. Be on alert for predators, morcougs, quartz lions, and whatever else," Aldis warned them.

Their stomachs full for the time being, they packed up and headed for the forest. It was actually quite beautiful, serene, enchanting almost, with its pretty trees and foliage. It was hard to imagine any predators lurking within.

They rode on steadily in single file. Aldis and Brenn had taken the lead. Erica wondered if they were traveling in the right direction. Everything looked the same to her. She had to trust they knew where they were going, so she concentrated instead on what had happened between her and Laro. *Lifemate? Really?* It was all so hard to believe. Once again, she thought she was hallucinating everything, that she was still on her ship and none of this was real.

"Erica?"

Laro's voice calling her name startled her out of her musings. "Yes?"

Laro gazed at her, concern in his eyes. "You looked almost asleep. You all right?"

"Yes, I'm fine. Does Aldis even know where we're going?"

"Yes, trust him. We'll be fine. We'll reach Zugut before sundown."

"I'm worried about my crew, Laro. And about the survivors from the Initiation Two." Not quite true. Her thoughts had been on him at that moment, not on the Initiation Two.

"I know you are, love. You can deal with it when we return."

"And what makes you think we'll return?"

"We will. The gods and goddesses are with us. We will succeed."

"How can you always be so optimistic with every..." The sky darkened, and crashes sounded through the forest, interrupting her. Erica gazed up. "What the fuck?"

Logs the size of houses rained from the sky, crashing to the ground, blocking their path and halting their advance. Erica clamped her legs around her saddle and tightened the reins as her horse reared up and whinnied. She sighed in relief as she gained control. She had no wish to repeat her plunge from the day before.

"Get closer together!" Ciara yelled.

Chanting reached Erica's ears as Icaras and Ciara cast a spell creating a barrier protecting them from the falling logs. Dismounting, they stayed close together within the safety of the shield. By the time the logs stopped crashing down, the forest around them was littered with them.

Icaras clenched his jaw. "He is growing more determined than ever to stop us."

Erica grasped Laro's hand as she gazed around. The huge

logs surrounded them, successfully caging them in. Above, all she could see were the broken tops of the trees. She hated to think of the damage to the forest. With the devastation that had happened on Earth, she couldn't understand why Zohmes chose to destroy such a beautiful place. *How are we going to be able to set things right?*

"Anyone have any ideas about how we are going to get out of this?" Ivran asked.

Erica gave Laro a sidelong glance. "Yes, optimistic one. Any ideas on how we are going to get the hell out?"

"Climb." Laro grinned at her, dimple flashing.

The air rushed out of Erica's lungs. *So damn sexy.* She glared at him. "You are *not* funny. How do you propose we get our horses over those mountainous logs? Haul them up with ropes?"

"Ropes? Ciara and I will cut through the trees using magick. I would suggest we lead the horses through. I'd rather they not suffer any injuries," Icaras said in a serious tone.

"It was meant sarcastically," Erica muttered.

"Icaras, using the magick you and Ciara expended to go back in time to draw us a map and the shield to protect us, you are already weakened," Brenn said.

"We have to try," Ciara said.

Icaras and Ciara joined hands, using their magick like a blade to cut through the logs blocking them in, then pushed them to the side, creating an opening. They led their horses through while Ciara and Icaras worked on the next log, and the next, so they could continue their progression through the debris.

Erica felt like they had been at it for hours. There was no way in hell they'd make it to Zugut before nightfall. How much longer could Icaras and Ciara keep this up before they collapsed? "Climbing might have been faster."

"What was that, love?" Laro chuckled.

"Nothing... nothing at all."

Erica swore as a root caught her foot. Stumbling, she landed on her knees. Could it get any worse? She felt the material of her pants rip and knew her knees had taken a beating.

Laro grasped her arm and pulled her to stand. "Are you hurt?"

The sharp sound of wood cracking echoed around them. The trunks of the fallen trees split open, with large rat-like creatures scurrying through the openings. There were so many of them, they reminded Erica of an army of ants. Very huge ants. Long tails swiped out as the creatures reared up, sniffing the air. Red beady eyes homed in on them. They had scented their prey.

"Oh, hell fucking no!" Erica reached for her fleet weapon only to find it missing. Where had she lost it? She grabbed her sword, holding it with both hands to keep from dropping it.

A warm body caged Erica from behind. Strong hands adjusted her grip. "Hold it like this, love," Laro said, then stepped away from her and grabbed his own sword.

She had to admit that the sword was easier to handle after he'd adjusted her grip. "Why in the hell are your creepy crawlies so fucking huge!"

"Icaras is shielding them from attacking us. I'm not sure how long he can hold them off, but we need to move. I'll continue cutting through the trees," Ciara said.

Erica saw how weary both Ciara and Icaras were growing. The rat swarm would overtake them in seconds as soon as the shield began to dissipate.

Ciara cut through another trunk and moved it. "Come on, we must hurry." She cut through trunk after trunk, enabling their party to move much faster through the maze of trees.

They moved at a steady pace, until Ciara stumbled and fell.

Brenn moved swiftly to catch her and gathered her to his chest. "She's not going to be able to keep this up. Ciara, you need to stop," he growled, his brow furrowed with worry.

Icaras wasn't faring any better. He looked pale, his forehead glazed with sweat, and Aldis was supporting his weight while Ivran led their horses.

The creatures scurried over the trunks of the huge trees, following them, waiting for the chance to strike. She shivered in revulsion. Laro pulled her into his arms. She relaxed against him, needing to feel his strength. There was no way in hell they were getting out of this alive. From the corner of her eye, she caught a flash of light. Her gaze followed the flash. Fires blazed around them, tall plumes of smoke curling upward. She closed her eyes against the rush of heat as Icaras dropped to his knees. The shield had broken.

Her heart hammered, knots of fear attacking her while she waited for the rodents to attack.

Nothing happened. No claws ripping her flesh to shreds. Cautiously, she opened her eyes. Two dragons had come. They swooped in like the cavalry, incinerating the monster rats, and blazed a trail to the outskirts of the town.

She watched as the dragons flew back, landed, and shifted. Taylith stood near Brenn and Ciara. The other dragon had turned into a blonde siren.

And now Taylith was handing Brenn his ass for putting Ciara in danger. Holy hell, was he pissed. And if that tall, lithe beauty with the long, silver hair turned her come-hither gaze one more time on Laro, she was going to rip every single strand of that hair from her beautiful head.

"Ciara cannot keep up this pace. You are asking too much of her," Taylith shouted, his forehead furrowed, his anger directed at Brenn.

Brenn brushed a lock of hair from Ciara's face, worry etched his features. "You better than anyone know how stubborn Ciara is when those she loves are in danger. I tried to warn her. She would not listen."

Aldis interjected. "We would have died, had Ciara and Icaras not stepped in. They saved us."

"Zohmes has been relentless. He is to blame for this, not us," Brenn added.

Taylith's blue eyes flashed to those of his dragon. "You had better take care of your mate or you will have to deal with me."

"Taylith, please, do not..." Ciara whispered before she lost consciousness.

Erica took a cloth out of her backpack, wet it from the waterskin, then knelt by Ciara and placed the cloth on her forehead. Slowly, she began to come to. She handed the cloth to Brenn, who continued to sponge Ciara's face, until she sat up.

Taylith caressed Ciara's cheek while still glaring at Brenn. "I suggest you rest now that the path is clear to Zulug. I will not tell your father of this."

"How did you know?" Ciara asked.

"Rania."

"Of course," Icaras muttered.

Taylith turned to Brenn again. "Take care of her. Never put her in such danger again, or you will regret it. Come, Tura, our work here is done."

Erica was glad the blonde moved away from Laro. She watched the dragons fly away and looked at Brenn's crestfallen face. Poor guy. It wasn't his fucking fault. "Why can't the dragons stay to help us?"

Ciara shook her head, seemingly regaining her strength fast. "Rania can only assist if her grandchildren or I are in grave danger. She felt Icaras and me weakening."

Erica heard the sound of gurgling water. "Could there be a river nearby?"

Brenn nodded. "I hear it, too. We're all exhausted. We will camp near the river for the night and continue to Zulug at sunup."

The river wasn't far from the trail the dragons had created. It wasn't an actual river. It was more like a gurgling stream, but the water looked clear. They set up camp, Laro helping with her tent.

Erica was glad she didn't have a mirror, because she knew she looked like hell. She smelled like smoke, and her hair felt like she hadn't bathed in weeks. Soot covered her from head to toe.

"Un-fucking-believable," Erica growled as she grabbed a bundle of clean clothing from her pack. Yes, they'd needed the help, and she was thankful for it, but the backwoods attitude had pissed her off. The tent flap opened as someone stepped in. "What?" she snapped.

"I am grabbing my pack and going further down the river to wash. If you would like to bathe, come with me," Laro said as he gently pulled her to her feet, wiped her cheek with his finger, and showed her the black smudge left behind. "Even though you are adorable covered in soot, I am not."

Erica slipped her arms around his waist and leaned against him. She sighed as his arms closed around her. "You're sexy covered in soot," she mumbled against his chest.

He chuckled, grabbed her hand, and pulled her out of the tent. "Your sword."

She sighed. "That thing is so heavy, and I still don't know how to use it properly."

"Bring it. There could be other predators hiding in the forest. After we eat, I'll give you another lesson."

CHAPTER ELEVEN

Erica struggled out of Laro's tight embrace. He still slept soundly, so she was careful not to wake him. The suns had risen above the horizon, the sky a bright pink, yellow, and orange. She shivered. She'd love nothing better than to crawl back in the sleeping bag and snuggle against his warmth, but she could hear movement in the campsite.

She left the tent and hurriedly relieved herself behind a nearby tree, then opened the flap of her tent to grab her jacket. Laro still slept, snoring softly. Gazing at his handsome face for a few moments, she sighed. *I'm falling crazily, head over heels in love with this man. A life with him by my side isn't all that unattractive to think about. But lifemates? I still can't come to terms with it all.*

Shaking the thoughts from her mind, she hurried to the crackling of a fire.

"There you are. We were waiting for you and Laro. We'll head to The Growling Lion, and we'll have breakfast there," Brenn told her as she approached.

"I'd better go and wake —"

"No need. I'm right behind you, wicked wench, letting me sleep."

She swiveled to face him and punched his arm. "Watch it. You'll find out how wicked I am!"

Laro grinned at her and rubbed his arm. "I look forward to it. I've packed up the tent and put your gear on the packhorse."

Brenn doused the fire with water from the stream, then buried the ashes with sand. Mounting, he led the way through the forest back to the trail the dragons had forged. It wasn't long before Erica saw houses and streets. The town resembled an old Wild West town. Her stomach rumbled, and she heaved a sigh of relief when she saw the sign dangling from a post, a large star with an etching of a growling lion in its center.

"We'll only be here to eat, so we won't need to stable the horses," Brenn told them as he dismounted and tied his horse to the post.

Erica suppressed a grin as she looked at the hitching post and a water-filled trough nearby. She dismounted and followed Brenn's example.

Aldis and Brenn led the way into the inn. The interior was rustic, again reminding her of pioneer days. It looked something like a saloon.

"Morning, travelers," the innkeeper greeted them.

The inn was almost empty. Two men and a woman sat at one of the tables. It was probably too early. Erica chose a stool at the bar. "I could stand a coffee right now," she muttered under her breath.

Ciara sat next to her and laughed. "I have taken a liking to this Earth liquid. I don't think the innkeeper can help us, though."

"What is on the menu for breakfast?" Ivran asked.

"Bit early, but Petronia is busy in the kitchen. She is making salted echidna, lodiomelo buns, roasted onnagus with ebocress, and yojitine."

"Sounds appetizing," Icaras said.

"Mead?"

Brenn grinned. "Bit early for that. How about sticky orb?"

"That sounds like something a child would drink. What is it?" Erica asked, pulling a face.

"It's quite a pleasant warm liquid often served in inns and taverns," Ciara explained.

"Okay. I'll try anything once."

"We'll have a full breakfast for all of us," Brenn told the innkeeper.

The man disappeared into what Erica presumed to be a kitchen. He returned carrying a tray with seven steaming mugs on it and set a mug on the bar for each. Erica sipped it carefully. "Mm, tastes like some kind of herbal tea. Not unpleasant."

"My name is Jazon. I've never seen you here before. Where are you headed?" the innkeeper said.

"We are looking for someone," Icaras replied.

"Someone here in Zulug?"

Fortunately, the cook interrupted the conversation. Erica was already wondering how Icaras could explain who they were in search of. "Saved by the bell."

Laro, who sat on the other side of her, questioned her. "Bell? What bell?"

She elbowed him. "Silly. Earth language. Okay, before I dig into this, what am I eating?"

Ciara giggled. "Nothing strange. It is good. Try it."

Erica cautiously took a bite. "As long as it's not rat meat."

"Rat?"

"Earth creature. A small version of those things that attacked us. The cities on Earth are overrun by rats. They carry diseases, but starving people will eat anything."

The meal was tasty, so Erica thought she'd better not ask more questions. While she ate, she listened to the conversation between the innkeeper and the cook who had come out of the kitchen. She seemed to be his mate.

"Jaleah came to deliver jago milk, butaro, and cheese this morning and of course had her imaginary daughter with her."

"Pretonia, why do you let it bother you? I am tired of

hearing stories about your sister and her mate and their invisible child. How long has it been now? Every day you annoy me with tales about that family."

"Who else can I talk to? I'm not going to spread around town that my sister and her husband are crazy."

"Look, as long as they deliver their wares, that's fine. That's all I want to hear... that they delivered their goods on time," Jazon said in a terse tone, making his annoyance clear to his mate.

"We earn quite a bit by selling the blankets their invisible daughter supposedly makes. And she *is* my sister. I still care for her even if she wants to pretend she has a child. Let them live their fantasy. You've got nothing to complain about. I bore you four young ones. So, stop it," Pretonia growled and returned to the kitchen.

Icaras pushed his plate away. "That was a good meal. You have a crazy farmer living nearby?"

Erica suppressed a giggle.

The innkeeper nodded and pointed to his forehead. "Crazy farmer and his mate. She's my mate's sister."

"You're a lion shifter," Brenn suddenly said.

The innkeeper looked startled. "Ssh. How do you know?"

"I just know. How about you tell us where to find that farm?"

"They don't like visitors. Why would you want to go there?"

"I see the blanket hanging on the wall. I like it and want to buy one for all of us. Unless you have more in stock?" Icaras said.

"Pretonia!" the innkeeper yelled into the kitchen. "How many of those blankets do we have?"

The woman appeared, wiping her hands on her apron. "How many do they want?"

"Seven," Brenn told her.

"I have two. If you come back in two days—"

"I want them now. Give us directions to your sister's farm, please?"

"She doesn't like any visitors. They live far away."

"Not far enough so that they can't deliver their wares here," Aldis said. "We are on a mission for King Biryn. We need those blankets. They look warmer than the blankets sold in the marketplace. Those mountains are very cold once we climb higher up."

The woman was hesitant until Brenn shoved seven gold coins across the bar. "Yours if you give us directions."

"Tell them," the innkeeper ordered.

Pretonia muttered something under her breath, then grabbed the coins greedily and yanked a napkin from the pile. She drew a little map and shoved it toward Brenn. "Half a day's ride. My sister leaves during the night to get here on time in the morning."

After mounting their horses, Erica said, "Those blankets were half the price of what you paid, Brenn."

Brenn gave her a half-smile. "It was worth it. We got directions out of them without any further argument."

"You took a risk. What if she'd had seven blankets?"

"I know. I suppose I would have bought them and found another way to get the information we need."

"I hope they were honest. What if the map leads us to nowhere?" Erica couldn't help but feel wary.

"They wouldn't dare, not after mentioning the king and seeing our swords strapped to our backs." Ivran looked as confident as Brenn.

"If all goes well, we could be there well before lunch. Our horses will travel faster than a horse-drawn wagon. Those travel almost at walking pace," Brenn mentioned.

"Let's head out," Aldis said.

Erica spurred her horse on. "Let's hope Zohmes doesn't

decide to bombard us with more logs... or giant rats." She shuddered in revulsion.

They rode quickly out of town, following the drawing on the map. Erica stayed on alert, watching their surroundings. Luckily, the damage from the logs wasn't as extensive as she'd feared. Zohmes had targeted the area they were riding all the way to the edge of the forest and had left the rest of the lush trees and landscape unaffected.

Relaxing her guard, she shifted in her saddle. Between the sword lessons and being thrown from her horse, she was sore as hell. Laro was a hard taskmaster, correcting her grip, her stance, teaching her several offensive and defensive moves before driving her to the brink of exhaustion in a mock sword fight. Then, later in her tent, he'd touched, kissed, and caressed every bruise and sore muscle, until she was liquid putty. Her body relaxed, she had drifted off to sleep snuggled in his arms. She took a deep breath and sighed. Yes, a life with him would be amazing, but what would her crew think? Would they accept her moving on and building something for herself? A new life? New beginnings? Mark's words filled her mind. *You are allowed to be happy, too.*

Laro's voice pulled her from her thoughts.

"Look up ahead. I think that may be the farmhouse."

The forest was thinning and up ahead she could see fields of grain and animals grazing in large pastures. A large, sprawling farmhouse stood in the far distance. "Should we be worried? After yesterday, I am finding it hard to believe we could be so lucky today."

They rode on, faster now that their destination was in clear sight. Approaching the ranch, they slowed the horses. A group of what looked and sounded like dogs played in a clearing a short distance from the house. "What are those?" Erica asked.

"They are koras. Great pets for children, but they also make good herding animals. Most farmers use them to herd their jagos," Laro explained.

"They resemble what we call a dog. They even sound similar. Oh, look, they're playing with a ball."

Ciara laughed. "A ball that stops in mid-air."

Erica watched the ball hover above the koras. They jumped up trying to get it, but it was too high. "Magic?"

Icaras dismounted and was about to walk to the animals when a door opened, and a shouting woman ran toward them. Waving a thick stick at them, she yelled, "Go away. We do not like strangers on our property. Rimog! Rimog! Come here!"

A man came running from the back of the house. "Jaleah, what is all the noise—"

"We are friends," Brenn said, slowly edging his horse on to approach the couple.

That gave Icaras the chance to walk closer to the animals and the ball still drifting above them. The koras nipped playfully at his legs. Slow but steady, he moved to the ball. When he was almost there, he reached out.

Erica gasped. A cloud of soft, shimmering particles appeared in front of Icaras. The particles began to solidify, and in seconds, a beautiful young woman faced Icaras, who was holding her wrist, her other hand holding the ball.

"His touch removed the invisibility spell," Ciara said.

The farmer and his mate ran to Cylena. "Get inside, girl. We will get rid of the strangers."

"No. He can see me."

Icaras reached out and took both her hands in his, the ball dropping to the ground. "Cylena, sister," he uttered.

The woman's hands flew to her face. "Rimog, she is visible?"

Ciara dismounted and walked to the couple, followed by Brenn. "We can see her. The young man is Icaras, her brother.

His touch broke the invisibility spell."

"And who are you?" the farmer asked.

"My name is Ciara, and this is my mate, Brenn. Behind me are our friends, Erica, Laro, Ivran, and Aldis. We have come a long way to find Icaras' sister."

Erica dismounted and walked among the nipping animals, followed by the others. "Does it feel real, Icaras?"

He shook his head. "I can't stop staring at her. Cylena, I am your twin brother. We were separated at birth." He let go of her hand and pulled the amulet out from beneath his tunic. He held it up.

Cylena's face was a picture of incredulity as she gazed at the amulet. Then she touched the one hanging on a chain around her own neck. The two amulets magically drew together and melded into one. Cylena and Icaras both now had a complete amulet depicting the face of their mother with two infants.

Looking at Icaras and Cylena standing together now, there was no doubt the two were twins, they were so much alike. Wavy black hair framed almost identical faces. Icaras' face was more manly of course, but Cylena resembled a feminine version of him. Cylena had not yet said a word nor moved at all beyond holding the amulet.

"My name is Rimog Eetu. This is my mate, Jaleah. We found Cylena abandoned beside the road many years ago. She was newly born. Jaleah is barren, and we believed the gods had smiled upon us and given us a child. We soon found her to be invisible to anyone but us, causing our family to think us stricken by madness. We love her like our very own. What does this mean now? Cylena has never been exposed to people."

"Cylena is meant to be with Icaras, her brother," Ciara told the anxious parents.

A loud whistling noise came from above. They looked up.

"Run!" Aldis shouted.

Erica looked up as she heeded his warning and ran. From the corner of her eyes she saw Icaras hustling his sister and her parents away from the house. A huge ball of fire came hurtling from the sky, heading straight for the farmhouse. It crashed into it, turning it into an inferno in seconds. Jaleah fainted, dropping to the ground at her mate's feet.

"Mother!" Cylena ran to the fallen woman.

Ciara walked away from them and called out her dragon. She blew and doused the flames, but there was little to nothing left of the house.

The farmer yanked at his long, graying hair in despair. "Our house! What magick is this? What have you brought upon us?" he shouted, turning angrily to face the group.

"There is much to tell," Ciara said after calling out her human.

Holding his sister's hand, Icaras joined them. "Cylena is coming with me to live in her rightful home. You are her mother and father, having raised her all these years. You are welcome in my castle."

"You destroyed our house. Why should we want to go with you or allow Cylena to?"

Jaleah had come out of her faint and joined him. "My beautiful house. It is all gone."

"We didn't destroy it. An angry god did."

"Who? Why?"

"Zohmes, a banished god. He did not want Icaras to find his sister," Ciara explained.

"Will this god harm our daughter?"

"With Icaras by her side, the god Zohmes cannot touch her."

Jaleah shook her head. "I do not understand."

"I've sent Dunmore the coordinates. He should be here shortly," Aldis interrupted.

"What about the horses?" Erica asked.

"We will unsaddle them and set them free. The same with the farm animals," Brenn answered.

Icaras approached the anxious couple, pulling Cylena with him. "Please, we need to leave here."

"We can stay at the inn with my sister and her mate," Jaleah argued. "Now that they can see Cylena, they will know we are not madness stricken."

Icaras frowned. "My sister needs to come with me."

"Father, Mother, I always knew something was missing in my life. There was an emptiness deep within in my heart. I never understood it, but now I do. I feel the bond with Icaras, a bond that only infants that shared their mother's womb can feel. Please, come with us?"

"Why was Cylena abandoned at birth? Who are your parents?" Rimog asked suddenly.

Erica saw Icaras' hesitation. "Cewrick. Our mother died after childbirth. Cewrick killed her and threw Cylena into the river to die. The goddess Rania saved her and placed her by the road. You were chosen by the gods to raise her and keep her safe."

"That evil sorcerer? That cannot be," Jaleah exclaimed.

"I'm afraid so. I defeated Cewrick. He hated me, but that is another long story," Icaras told them.

"The hovercraft is here," Aldis announced as it landed.

"Are you coming with us?" Cylena asked her parents.

Erica watched the horses gallop off toward the forest, along with the herd of jago and other animals Laro and Ivran had freed.

Rimog looked at his mate. "There is nothing left for us here."

"No, and I do not want to be parted from my daughter. Yes, we will go with you, though I would rather travel on the road," Jaleah answered, still showing some reluctance.

CHAPTER TWELVE

The flight to Brenn's estate had not taken long, and during it, they had tried to explain as much as they could to Jaleah and Rimog, while Icaras talked to Cylena.

Erica looked at Icaras' happy expression. He had been a lonely boy, then sent to live as a giant worm, so he'd had a solitary life. Right now, he had to feel great that he had a sister, some family of his own. She watched him talking softly to her, the expression on Cylena's face just as happy, and by the looks of it, she was going to adore her brother and dote on him.

A fierce longing invaded her thoughts, a yearning for a family of her own, children, even one child, she could love, hug, and cuddle. A husband... Laro.

"Erica?" He took her hand in his and squeezed it. "You all right?"

She rested her head on his shoulder. "Just tired."

"I will drop you all off and go home. I'll send a report to the king," Aldis told them.

Rimog and Jaleah had never traveled that far, so they had never seen the big city or the wealthy estates on its outskirts. They exclaimed in wonder when they stood in the courtyard.

"Please, follow us," Ciara told the couple.

"One of my staff will show you to your rooms where you

can refresh for dinner," Brenn said.

"They'll need clothing, Brenn. They have nothing left," Ciara reminded him.

"Right. I'll send word to the seamstress to deliver clothes forthwith. Can you get their measurements?"

"Can she sew that fast?" Erica questioned.

Brenn laughed. "She sells her clothing at the markets, so she has a good supply that is ready. By the time they finish bathing, their clothes will be waiting for them."

The aroma of something roasting on the barbecue was strong in the air when they entered the house. Erica realized she was hungry, but more than anything, she needed to relax in a hot bath.

Icaras turned to them before heading to his room. "Thank you all for your help. I am forever in your debt. I will have to thank Aldis, too. I have a great idea. We will have a grand celebration for the return of my sister. Maybe at my castle?"

"Sounds good," Brenn said.

Laro accompanied Erica to her door. "I will see you at dinner, my love. I ache for a bath as much as you."

Relaxing in the warm bath, allowing the oils she'd added to soothe her aching muscles, her mind drifted to her crew and the survivors of the Initiation Two. Tomorrow she would talk with the crew and check on the survivors. It was going to be tough. She hated discontent and what it could breed.

Laro's banging on the door caused her to quickly wash and climb out of the bath. Wrapping a towel around her, she answered. "Where's the fire?"

He came in with a sheepish grin on his lips. "Dinner is ready. You took a long time."

Erica stood on the tip of her toes and wrapped her arms around his neck. Damn, he was hard to resist. She nipped his chin. "Let me get dressed."

He tilted her chin up, kissing her gently. "Hurry, my

precious," he murmured against her lips as he slid his hands down her shoulders and back to grasp her ass. She gasped as he pulled her up against him. "We have about ten minutes before my son gets bored with the adults downstairs and comes searching for us."

She gazed up at him and giggled. "He wouldn't, would he?"

He kissed the tip of her nose. "Yes, he would. He is anxious to see you."

Erica smiled. It filled her with joy to think that Tomas had missed her. He had wriggled his way into her heart as rapidly as his father. "Then let's not keep him waiting."

Erica dressed quickly and walked with Laro to join the others at dinner. Before they made it halfway to the dining room, Tomas rounded the corner and bounded to them, a bright smile on his face. She couldn't help but giggle as Laro gave her a pointed look.

"Everybody is outside. The cook let me help set up the tables."

"Well, come on, then. We don't want to keep them waiting." Erica smiled as Tomas grabbed her hand and led them to the courtyard where the others were waiting.

Catching sight of Laura and Mark, Erica turned to Laro. "Give me a minute? I need to talk to Mark. I won't be long."

Laro squeezed her hand. "Come on, sprout. Let's go find a seat."

Erica grinned as her gaze followed them to the table. Tomas had seated himself so she would be between them.

She glanced up to catch Mark smiling at her. "You look very happy, Erica. It suits you."

"Did everything go smoothly while I was away? How are the survivors of the Initiation Two crew?"

"Everything went well with job placements. The king's steward worked to place the crew within the city so we would be close to each other. I agree with his decision. As for the Initiation Two, Aria is now in stable condition but still in the hospital. She's at least out of intensive care. The others are in good health and have been transferred to the compound," Mark updated her.

Erica sighed in relief. "Good. I am glad to hear they are doing well. Too many were lost in the crash." Pain stabbed her heart as she thought of Hannah. "And you? Have you decided what you would like to do?"

"Actually, I asked to join Brenn's troops. He granted my request this evening as well as Laura's request to remain here for the time being. She feels safe in Brenn's house. It will take time for her to get over her fear," Mark said.

"I thought you'd make the request to join Brenn. Thank you for handling things while I was away. I'll be meeting with the crew tomorrow to check on everyone."

Erica was relieved that the plans for her crew had gone so smoothly. Now that the crew had a path for their future, maybe the discontent would be alleviated.

Laura glanced at Erica with pain-filled eyes. "Erica, do you mind if I go with you to the compound? I think it would be better if I told Julia in person that I'll be staying here for a while. She's refused my communications."

Erica clasped Laura's hands. "Of course, Laura. But are you sure? I can tell her if you aren't comfortable leaving the estate."

"I'm sure. I've been visiting Aria in the hospital with Mark. It's helped with my fear some."

"That's good to hear. Let's join the others. I see Brenn's staff is starting to bring out the food, and I'm starved after the long day we've had."

Erica seated herself between Laro and Tomas. Laro clasped her hand in his. "Everything fine?" he asked.

She glanced up at him, longing for dinner to end swiftly.

All she wanted to do was to slip back to her room and lose herself in his arms. "Everything is fine, I think. I'll meet with the crew tomorrow morning to get a better handle on things."

Dinner was relatively quiet, but a distinctive undertone of happiness simmered in the room. Talk of Zohmes had been pushed aside for the night as they just relaxed and enjoyed the success of their mission and the company of friends and family. Even Jaleah and Rimog seemed quite at ease, and Cylena sat next to Icaras, gazing at him with adoration. Erica couldn't help but smile at the people gathered around the table. For once, she didn't feel like she was an outsider looking in. She felt as if she had finally come home.

Erica giggled as Laro pulled her into her room and shut the door. Lifting her, he carried her to the bed and gently set her on the comforter. She grabbed him by the shirt to pull him down beside her. Her pulse kicked into high gear as he captured her mouth with his in a kiss that seared her to her soul.

Laro broke away and quickly divested himself of his clothing. Erica yanked hers off as well, never taking her attention off his body. He stood beside the bed, staring down at her as she lay naked. Love shone from his eyes. Oh, he was gorgeous, this giant of a man, and he was a giant in more ways than one. His cock pulsed against his abdomen, big, fully erect. She spread her legs, feeling her clit pulsate as he fixed his gaze on her pussy. "Come," she invited and held out her arms.

He was beside her in a second. That was not what she wanted. She needed him to fill her. That magnificent tool needed to pierce her to her core. She tried to pull him on top, but he would have none of it. A shuddering sigh escaped her lips as he bent, his lips stroking her forehead, down her nose, resting briefly on her lips, then down her neck to her breasts.

He kneaded each breast and nibbled at her nipples before trailing down her body to her clit. He sucked hard. She moaned as he ignited a fire within her like she'd never felt in her life.

Reaching down, she entwined her fingers in his long hair and pushed his head hard against her folds. He lapped the juices from between, then sat on his knees and gazed down at her. Erica lifted her hips, opening completely up to him. He took his cock in his hand and guided the head to her waiting opening but didn't enter right away. He rubbed it between her folds, played with the entrance, before finally inching in.

"You are so tight, starshine," he said softly.

Her body ravenous with need, she captured the lean muscles of his ass, urging him on. "Take me! Please, take me now!"

With one last push he entered. She gasped as his cock filled her completely. He began to thrust, then gathered her into his arms and claimed her lips. Erica wrapped her legs around him, pulling him into her as hard as she could.

"I can't hold it! I'm coming!" she yelled as her body began to tremble and she felt the release building to its crescendo. In response, his body shuddered. He groaned softly as they rode that final crest.

Breathing heavy, they lay in each other's arms for a few minutes until Laro rolled to her side. Erica leaned on an elbow and gazed down at him. "I love you, Laro. Yes, I will be your lifemate, but you'll need to explain what it all means. You already told me you will give me part of your soul. Will there be a ceremony like Brenn and Ciara's?"

His eyes sparked with joy. "Yes, my starshine. At the Clyss. It won't be quite the same, but that's where we will join."

"Starshine. How did you come up with that? I like it."

"When you gaze at me, your eyes light up like the brightest star."

She toyed with a lock of his hair. "Does everyone on Ierilia get married at the Clyss?"

"No. That is reserved for certain clans and only those that have found their lifemates. The people from Xynnar, the jewel dragons, and now that Cewrick is gone, I believe Icaras and his sister will be permitted to go there."

Erica giggled.

"Why are you laughing while we are having a serious talk?" Laro said, annoyance written on his face.

"I'm sorry. A thought occurred to me, and it made me laugh. A lot of customs on Ierilia are completely foreign to us Earthlings. I'm so glad you have normal sex."

He frowned. "Sex. Such a harsh word for two people joining and expressing their love. Did you imagine it to be different from how you join on Earth?"

"Honey, the thought never occurred to me until now. That's why I giggled."

"Honey?"

Erica sighed. "An Earth endearment. Honey is actually something we spread on bread or sweeten coffee or tea with. It's very sweet."

"You have made me a very happy man tonight," Laro murmured against her cheek.

"I'm just as happy. After everything I loved was ripped from me on Earth, I never thought I could find happiness again. Those three words *I love you* are just empty words. You have become the light inside of me. My time on Earth will be merely a memory, some of it precious, other memories not so much."

"And you occupy my heart and my soul, my Erica. Please, do not ever change. You are the strongest woman I have ever known. You can be soft and sweet in my arms, but always be the woman I first fell in love with."

"What puzzles me, your gods sometimes pick your

lifemates. How is it that they would have picked me for yours? A woman from Earth?"

"The gods know all, past, present, and future."

"So they knew my ship would crash on Ierilia and your lifemate aboard it?"

"Yes. And now, my starshine, we need to rest. You have a task to attend to in the morning."

Snuggling into his arms, she rested her head on his shoulder. "Goodnight, lover."

CHAPTER THIRTEEN

"**M**ark, will you go with me and Laura to the compound after breakfast?" Erica drank her jago milk.

Mark gave her a lopsided grin. "Is that an order, Captain?"

"Don't be silly. I'm giving you the option, but honestly, yes, I would like you to be there."

"Then I will go with you."

"Great. Brenn said he'll fly us there. I've already contacted Julia to have the whole crew gathered in the common room along with the survivors of the Initiation Two."

Laura stared at her quizzically. "You're not wearing your uniform?"

"No. Now that I have a commission in Brenn's troops, my Earth uniform will be a relic, history. This is who I am now."

After Erica had returned from their mission, she'd found her army uniforms and gear had been delivered to Brenn's estate. She wore her daily uniform of black leather-like pants and a form fitting black shirt with a rounded collar that came to the base of her throat. Her rank as captain was embroidered in gold thread around the collar. Black, knee-high boots covered her feet and legs, and her sword was strapped to her back. The outfit made her feel like a ninja.

"I love that sword. Can you imagine that on Earth? It would be worth a fortune. Can I hold it?" Laura inquired.

"Sure." Erica pulled her sword from the scabbard and handed it to Laura.

Laura held it as if it were made of glass. Gently, she stroked the blade. "I wonder what all these symbols mean."

"Very few have such a sword. Brenn has one, and the king. I felt very honored when the king gave it to me at the ceremony. It's like receiving a gold medal on Earth. It's precious, and Brenn told me it's infused with magic. His people made it."

Laura sighed. "Wow. I can only wish."

Erica laughed. "And pray tell me, what would you do with a sword?"

"Hang it on the wall. It's too beautiful to use. And don't forget, we were all trained to defend ourselves."

"But not by using a sword such as that one," Mark interrupted and snickered.

Laro joined them. "We are all late this morning. Why didn't you wake me, wench?" He kissed her on the cheek.

Erica laughed while placing the sword back into the scabbard. "You were sound asleep."

Icaras and Brenn came in and sat at the table. "We all deserved a good night's rest." Brenn began to load up his plate.

"Brenn, I was thinking last night. It might be too early to take my sister and her parents to the castle. Would it be too much to ask if we can have the celebration here?"

Ciara joined them. "That's a good plan. Having it at the castle might be too overwhelming for Cylena and her parents."

Brenn clapped him on the back. "Of course. When would you like to have it?"

Icaras spoke in a rush. "Tomorrow evening? Can we invite the king? And everyone involved in my rescue, defeating Cewrick, and finding my sister. Of course your parents, Ciara.

Maybe you can plan this for me?"

Ciara winked at Brenn then led Icaras to the table. "Of course I will. What about the Earth people?"

"Yes, of course. I am so excited."

Erica smiled. Icaras looked every bit an adult, a handsome rogue, but deep inside he was still the boy Cewrick had banished. The man had missed so much of his young life. "I'm finished. Are you ready, Laura? Mark?"

She stroked Laro's cheek, then left the kitchen to go to the waiting flyer, Laura and Mark right behind her.

It took hardly any time to arrive at the compound. Brenn had asked if he should accompany her, but Erica had politely declined. It would be better if she met with her crew alone.

Upon entering the common room, she found most of her crew seated at a long table. A small group sat huddled in a corner of the room and looked to be in a serious discussion. "Good morning, everyone."

"Captain," several of them greeted her. The ones in the corner looked startled. They stood and came to the table.

"It's nice of you to grace us with your presence finally, along with Mark and Laura." Sarcasm laced John's tone.

"It must be nice to be living in the lap of luxury while we're holed up in what's no better than a jail," Julia snapped.

"Enough! Sit!" Erica ordered.

"What gives you the right to order us? You're no longer our captain," John said and still stood.

Jill pulled back from the table. "You took a commission in the king's army. Mark told us. So yeah. We don't have to listen to you."

Erica felt her heart sink. The anger coming from some of her crew members felt overwhelming.

Mark's shoulders stiffened. "The captain will always be our captain, no matter what position she's taken here on

128

Ierilia."

Several of her crew nodded their assent.

"Fine. Remain standing then if that makes you feel more comfortable." She pulled out a chair and sat, looking at each of them. "Let's find out who is unhappy here. Hands please?"

She counted seven. John, Jill, Donna, Julia, Megan, Ronald, and Gary. The group that had been huddled together in the corner. "I'd like to welcome the survivors of the Initiation Two. Of course, you're not in a position yet to know what your feelings are about Ierilia and its customs."

Travis stood and looked at his fellow survivors. "We're just fucking grateful these people rescued us. If it hadn't been for them, we'd still be in stasis and would have died eventually as the computers gave out. All of us feel the same, even Aria, who can't wait to be discharged from the hospital."

John shot her an angry glower. "They have such advanced technology. I don't see why they can't give us a spaceship so we can continue our journey."

"John, be reasonable. This is a different universe. From what we've learned, there are no habitable planets for us in this expanse of space. Their ships travel in this universe only," Laura said calmly.

"Why not let us make our own way," Julia said.

"And go where?" Erica asked.

"I've studied their universe. There are quite a few planets besides Toubos and Ierilia. Surely one of those could sustain us?" Megan added.

"And start a new life with only seven of you? Gimme a break," Erica said, trying to contain her anger.

Mark stepped in. "The Ierilians have explored every inch of this universe and have found no planets that can sustain life for us or them. The few planets that have life on them, the aliens need to wear special gear to adapt to Ierilia and vice versa. We were damn fucking lucky to have crashed here where we can breathe and live a normal life."

"Ha ha ha! Normal?" Ronald continued to laugh.

"We're living in fucking medieval times," Gary contributed. "And as Julia said earlier, you're living in luxury while we're holed up here."

"Mark gave you all your commissions and said you accepted them." She looked at each questioningly.

"We did. At least it will get us out of here," Julia said.

"Right. And you've all been given new accommodations close to each other. Well, at least the Initiation Five crew has. You guys will need to learn the language and their ways first," she added, looking at the Initiation Two crew.

"Captain, do you think any more of our ships could have crashed here?" Olivia asked.

"I've pondered that possibility myself. I don't think it was a single asteroid. It could have been a belt. If so, other ships might not have made it through. Only time will tell, if ever. There are many unexplored regions on Ierilia. I'm going to speak to Brenn and find out if they have a way to track any crashed spaceships. Ierilia is a large planet, ten times the size of Earth," Erica told her.

"Like Travis, I'm glad to be alive and thankful to the Ierilians. They seem very hospitable," Olivia said.

"Oh, more than hospitable. Tell them about your love life, Captain!" Sarcasm almost drooled from Julia's lips.

"Julia! I can't believe I'm hearing this from my own sister. What the hell is wrong with you? Where is all this coming from?" Laura's eyes brimmed with tears.

"John talked some sense into us," Julia told her sister.

Erica sighed. John had shown rebellion from the beginning. "John, is this true?"

"Someone had to do a wakeup call. I'm going to do my damnedest to find a way to get off this hellhole of a planet. And they're going with me." He pointed at the other rebels.

"We're here. It is what it is, and Ierilia is a beautiful, peaceful planet. It doesn't need this discontent, this rebellion. I suggest you think long and hard about what you're saying and doing. We are citizens here now and not above their law."

"You just go and play with your lover and your sorcerer and dragons and your fancy sword. Leave us be," he snapped at her.

Erica saw the anger in his expression, and was she right? Was that utter hatred? She knew he was rebellious and had trouble adjusting to Ierilia and its customs, but to that extent? This didn't seem at all like the John she'd trained with on Earth.

Laura pushed her chair back and stood. She slowly approached her sister and held out her arms. "Jules? Honey? Please, what's wrong?"

Erica's heart broke for Laura as Julia pushed her away. "Tomorrow you'll all be transported to your new homes. I've seen them. The houses are small, big enough for two, so you can choose who to share with. The kitchens are stocked with food, and you've already been given clothing. You'll also be starting your new jobs and earning a living."

"While you still live in luxury," Julia snapped.

"I don't live in Brenn's house. I'm a guest. As long as he needs me for the quests or other missions, I'll be staying there. After that, just like you, I will have a place of my own. Have you all forgotten what it was like on Earth? Oh, right... you were all living in luxury there, weren't you?"

Erica thought she saw a fleeting expression of shame on several of the faces, but it disappeared fast. "By the way, there will be a celebration at Brenn's estate tomorrow night. You're all invited."

"Wow. Really?" Talia said. "Damn, what am I going to wear? My clothes were all destroyed in the crash."

"How do we get there?" Greyson asked.

Erica forced a smile. "You'll be transported with flyers. Be prepared to be awed. Their celebrations are something else."

"I'm not going." John glared at her and looked at his fellow rebels.

"Well, I am. Brenn puts on a great feast," Julia said.

"And this celebration is for what reason?" John asked.

"You don't even know yet. We found Icaras' sister. This is to celebrate the reunion of two siblings parted at birth."

"Oh, great. As if one sorcerer isn't enough. I presume the sister is a sorceress?"

Erica was getting very tired. "I really don't know. We just found the young woman. I suggest you pull your act together, John. Be thankful that we're alive. Look at how many perished on the Initiation Two. Twenty-five crew members lost their lives. That could have been us."

John finally shut up, but his lips were set in a grim line, and his eyes shot sparks of hatred at her.

"You'll all be given new communicators when you set out on your own. You can contact me at any time. Now, let's talk about your various job postings."

The chatter began. Erica was at least happy that there were only seven rebels among her crew. It could have been worse. John could have planted seeds of rebellion in all. How was she going to deal with the discontented crew members? At that point, she had no idea. Laura sat quietly beside her. Erica felt her pain at Julia's behavior. She stood and walked to Travis. "Travis, I'm so sorry about Hannah. I know you two were very close."

He stood and embraced her. "Yes, we were. Closer than anyone knew." He stepped back and took both her hands in his. "I gather from gossip you've found someone to share your life with?"

"I did. Never thought I'd find the love of my life on an alien planet," she told him and grinned.

"Most of the people look just like us. Well, the men are all bigger, taller. I don't know what those over there are so uptight about. They should be eternally grateful they're alive and on a beautiful planet. I haven't seen much of it yet, but from what I have, it's quite something."

Erica nodded. "Thankfully, most are of the same mindset. They'll begin to realize it soon."

"I hope so. John is the instigator," he informed her softly.

"I know. He was somewhat rebellious from the beginning, but now he seems like an entirely different person. We'll have to work on him. I'll see you tomorrow night. Brenn's flyer just landed, so I guess it's time to leave."

On the way back, Mark said, "You're both disturbed. I can feel it."

"To say the least. I'm so sorry, Laura. I don't understand what has gotten into Julia. Or John, for that matter."

Brenn landed the flyer and waited for them to exit. He joined Erica as they headed for the house. "What happened? Laura looks so unhappy."

Erica told him about her insubordinate crew members. "I don't quite know how to deal with it."

"Maybe Ciara can help. We'll talk to her."

"Magic?"

He grinned. "Well, it has its uses."

CHAPTER FOURTEEN

I caras took Cylena and her parents on a tour of the town and surroundings while Brenn's staff prepared the house for the celebration. Erica had not yet had a chance to talk to Ciara. The dragon princess was very much acting the lady of the house and organizing everything.

The great room and dining hall were already decorated with sparkling lights and garlands of flowers, and the smell of succulent foods wafted through the air from the kitchens and the smokers outside.

Damn, Talia wasn't the only one that needed something to wear. The only dress Erica had was the green one she had worn to the ceremony. She hurried to her room to change from her uniform. Maybe by the time she got changed, she could speak to Ciara about her crew and figure out where to get a dress for Talia.

She entered her room, dropped her pack, and closed the door. Gazing at her bed, she gasped. Laid out on her comforter was a dress with reddish-brown skirts that almost matched the color of her hair. Walking to the bed, she touched the soft material and smiled. The top had a cream undershirt with a scooped neck, long, flowing sleeves, and a corselet to match the reddish brown of the overskirts. Beneath the sea of brown peeked a red satin underskirt. It was by no means a frilly style. It was exactly what she would have picked out.

She grinned as she noticed a pair of matching shoes sitting beside the dress.

Erica pulled herself away from her bed and quickly changed from her uniform. She grabbed her sword to put it away with her fleet weapons but instead withdrew it from the scabbard. Setting the scabbard aside, she gazed at the beautiful scrollwork etched in the blade. It truly was a work of art, but was it magic? She hadn't felt or seen any magic from the blade yet. She had only handled it a couple of times on the mission and during her sword fighting lessons with Laro. She took a cleaning cloth from her closet and carefully wiped the smudges from the blade left by Laura's handling of it. Erica gasped as the etchings in the sword began to glow slightly. A tingling sensation ran through her body, then abruptly stopped. Maybe it really was infused with magic. Erica placed the sword back in the scabbard and carefully put it away in the closet, along with the cleaning cloth.

She dressed quickly and headed out to the courtyard to find Laro. Obviously, the man knew exactly where she could find a dress and shoes for Talia. She couldn't help but smile.

Erica found Laro sitting on a bench in the garden, quietly talking to Tomas. She slid on the seat beside them and leaned against Laro's strong shoulder. "Am I interrupting?"

"Is it true, Erica? Are you and Father going to get mated?" Tomas asked, a serious tone in his voice.

"You don't mind, do you? I love you both, Tomas, and I don't want to hurt you in any way," Erica said.

Tomas grinned at her and engulfed her in a hug. "I don't mind at all. I love you, too, Erica." He turned to Laro. "It's about time you found me a mother. I'm going to go help Kira in the orchard," he said as he took off out into the garden.

Tomas' comment had warmed the cockles of her heart. His reaction had been a relief. He'd had Laro to himself for so many years now. His words showed how much he had missed a mother figure in his life. She smiled up at Laro. "Thank you for the dress. Do you think you can help me find one suitable for Talia?"

Laro stood, pulling her up with him. "The dress looks lovely on you. You look good enough to eat. The seamstress is already on her way to the compound with several dresses. Kira suggested that the women of your crew might want to pick something for the party when I picked out the dress for you."

"I will have to thank Kira," she said, relieved that at least one task was off her list. "I have to find Ciara and see if she can help me with some of my crew."

Erica told him about her rebellious crew members, the way Julia had treated Laura and the outright hatred spewing from John.

Laro grimaced. "You may have to wait until after the celebration to talk to her. Your crew will settle down, starshine. The celebration has her well occupied. Stop worrying. Just imagine if I, or Brenn, were stranded on Earth. I think we'd be desperately unhappy."

"Eh, hardly a comparison, knowing the state Earth is in."

"True. Okay, on a different planet, then. Not everyone can adapt easily. Give them time."

She grabbed him by his hair, tugged his head down and kissed him. "You are the voice of reason. With all this going on, Zohmes has been far from my mind, but I don't trust the quiet. He must realize by now that Icaras' pendant is now whole. By the way, does Cylena have magical powers, too? Is she a sorceress?"

Laro drew her into his arms. "I would think she does. That's a question you'll have to ask Ciara."

"Talking about Ciara, I need to go find her." Erica moved away from him, playfully punched his arm, and headed into the house.

"Ciara, it is almost time for everyone to start arriving. Anything you would like me to do?" she asked as she approached the beautiful princess. And actually, she could find no words to describe her beauty. Ciara stood near the entrance, dressed in a deep purple gown edged with silver embroidery. As always, her black hair cascaded to her waist, but it seemed as if her union with Brenn had created a glow on her face that almost appeared as if she'd applied makeup, whereas women on Ierilia didn't wear makeup. Erica wondered if they even knew about such things.

"Thank you, Erica. Everything is ready. You look lovely. That dress really brings out your coloring, your hair and green eyes," she said. "Stand here with me to greet the guests. Your crew will appreciate it."

Erica heard the musicians strike up a tune. Their music drifted throughout the house. Brenn had some kind of hidden sound system that he could turn on and off at will. Their technology still baffled her, and their lifestyle. Medieval in many ways, yet so far advanced beyond Earth technology. Oh, but what scientists on Earth could learn from them. Deep down, she kind of wished the Ierilians could travel beyond their universe, take them back to Earth, with all of their knowledge. Alas, that could never be. Well, never say never. Maybe another thousand years into the future?

"Erica? Your crew is arriving," Ciara said, startling her out of her thoughts.

They filed in, John the second one to arrive. Erica was glad he had worn Ierilian clothing. The thought had occurred to her that he could arrive in his full officer's uniform. Talia looked cute in her dark pink overdress and frilly underskirt and blouse. All her crew looked very much like Ierilian nobility.

The king arrived last. Erica curtsied. "Your Majesty."

"Captain Martinez, how lovely to see you. We owe you so

much more than just a sword," he greeted her.

She and Ciara followed the king and his entourage into the dining hall, where the feast was already in full swing. Soon as she could, Erica escaped to find Laro.

She finally found him chatting amiably with Icaras. Cylena stood by his side, her arm linked through her brother's.

Erica's pulse kicked up a notch at the sight of him. Damn, he was dashing. His brown hair hung loose around his shoulders. A smile played across his face and that dimple of his wreaked havoc with her hormones. His clothing reminded Erica of a pirate's. The only thing missing was a scimitar. "Laro, here you are. I was looking all over for you."

"Icaras and I were in an interesting conversation about his time in the caves."

"Hardly a suitable conversation at a celebration," Erica muttered. "Cylena, how does it feel to suddenly be exposed to the world?"

Cylena smiled shyly. "It is overwhelming. It will take time for me to adjust."

"I can imagine that." Erica glanced up and smiled as Ciara made her way toward them with the king on her arm, his gaze on Cylena.

"King Biryn, I'd like to introduce you to Cylena, the goddess Rania's granddaughter and Icaras' sister."

Cylena curtsied, bowing her head. "Your Majesty. I am honored to be introduced."

Cylena gasped as King Biryn lifted her hand and kissed her fingertips. "My lady, would you do the honor of dancing with me?"

"I have never danced before, but yes, I would like to learn," Cylena said.

Erica smiled as King Biryn led Cylena to the dance floor. The king couldn't take his eyes off the girl. He looked positively smitten.

She emptied her goblet and set it down. "Come dance with me, Laro." As she laced her fingers with his and pulled him toward the other dancers, she noticed John dancing with Olivia. His gaze seemed riveted on her. She could hardly concentrate on Laro and the dancing. Was it her imagination or did she see a red glow in John's eyes? He almost appeared demonic. She shook her head and looked up at Laro.

Laro captured her gaze, his eyes full of concern. "What's wrong, starshine? Your mind isn't on dancing."

"I don't know. I guess I'm still worried about yesterday when I talked to the crew."

"Come on then. It will make you feel better if you mingle with them. To talk to them in a less formal setting."

Erica let Laro lead her from the dance floor to several members of her crew. Leaning down, he gently kissed her cheek. "I'm going to check on Tomas."

"Thank you." She smiled and turned to greet her crew members. "Is everyone enjoying the party?"

"We're having a great time. Everyone has been very courteous, and I think some of us are starting to make friends with some of the people here," Catrice said.

"I agree. I'm enjoying myself," Travis added.

She heard agreement from the others and smiled. Relieved that they were enjoying themselves, she continued around the room, speaking to her crew members. Each one looked like they were having a good time. Maybe she was overreacting.

As she made her way to the dining room to get something to drink, John stopped her. "Captain? Can I talk to you?" Erica was surprised. He appeared much more relaxed, and his eyes weren't shooting flames. Maybe she had just imagined it? "Sure, John. What can I help you with?"

"I wanted to tell you that I'm sorry for the way I acted yesterday. I know my behavior was appalling. I'd like to start over if that's okay?"

Erica looked at him. John behaved like he was sincere. And after talking with her crew, what had happened yesterday seemed to be pushed from their minds. "I appreciate that. I know if you give it a chance, you can have a good life here."

"Do you mind if I ask you a few questions? This place reminds me of a fairy tale. Some of the things we've seen or people we've met, like at the last party I met that pretty little lady with the wings and long, golden hair. Niqine, I think her name was. Was she a fairy? I haven't seen her tonight."

Erica smiled. "I thought the same thing when I met her. She was invited, but she doesn't like these large gatherings."

"I heard she was trapped in a cave and guarded some kind of book. I think you were on that mission, weren't you? I'd love to hear about it and where you found her," John probed.

Laro approached, carrying two glasses of wine. "Sorry to interrupt, Erica. I thought you could use something to drink," he said as he handed her the glass.

Erica laughed. "That was actually where I was headed before I ran into John." Turning to John, she added, "Do you mind if we talk later?"

"No problem, Erica. I think I'm going to find myself a dance partner," John answered, leaving to walk toward the ballroom.

Erica glanced up at Laro. "I think that went better than I thought it would. You were right. It did help to talk to them."

A slow tune began in the ballroom. Smiling at her, Laro took their glasses and set them on a table. "Good, now maybe we can enjoy that dance."

Erica let him guide her to the dance floor and pull her into his arms. She gazed around the room as he twirled her, her heart lighter after speaking with her crew. Many of them were on the dance floor or mingling with the Ierilians. They seemed to be adjusting well after their meeting. Laro swirled her, and she caught sight of the king. Cylena, Icaras, and John stood beside him. Surprisingly, John appeared to be in a discussion with Icaras. Closing her eyes, she relaxed against Laro to enjoy the last of the dance.

The music sped up again, and Erica tried to teach Laro an Earth dance. It caused a lot of mirth as the others tried to copy.

The food, the wine, the exhaustion of their mission, it was all beginning to take its toll. Erica had no idea what time it was. The clock was so different on Ierilia. She'd continued to wear her watch, but there was no comparison. Their days and nights were longer. And she'd not had the luxury of studying as her crew had.

Leaning heavily against Laro, she said, "I need to go to the bathroom. I'll be back shortly."

She went to her room and fell back onto the bed. All she really wanted to do now was sleep, but she knew she couldn't. It would be an insult if she didn't go back to the celebration. Heaving a sigh, she got off the bed, relieved herself, then walked to the closet and opened it. She just wanted a peek at her reward, her beautiful sword.

The sword wasn't there. The scabbard hung empty in her closet. That sobered her up instantly. Frantically, she searched her room, closets, drawers, pulling the covers off the bed. She checked under the bed. No sword. Anywhere. A sick feeling attacked her stomach. The sword was so special. For her to lose it would be a major insult to the king. "Dammit. I didn't lose it. I know I put it in the closet," she muttered.

Frustrated, she slammed the closet doors shut and left the room. Hurrying back to the celebration, she looked for Laro and finally found him in the dining room helping himself to more food. Tugging at his sleeve, she said, "Laro, I need to talk to you. Now. It's important."

He followed her away from the guests to a quiet side of the room and looked at her, concern filling his eyes. "What is so important? Is everything fine with your crew?"

Damn, she was going to sound incompetent. Nothing else had been touched in her room. "My sword is missing."

Laro scowled at her. "Where did you leave it last?"

"It was in the scabbard and I put it in my closet with my fleet weapons. The scabbard is still there, but my sword is gone. I think it's been stolen," Erica said in a rush. She knew someone had to have taken it. There was no other explanation. But who?

"Maybe you forgot where you put it, my love. It can't just be gone."

"Stop. I'm not stupid, and I'm not drunk or senile."

"What is senile?"

"Oh, for fuck's sake."

Laro clasped her hand in his. "Slow down, Erica. I know you're agitated, but why would anyone want to steal your sword?"

Erica took a deep breath to calm herself. "Maybe because it's special? It's magic? Or something. Damn, I don't know. Help me here!"

Laro pulled her out of the dining room and back to the party. "Come, we need to speak to Brenn. If your sword was stolen, it would have to be someone that knows the layout of his estate. Someone who knows where your room is."

They found Brenn and Ciara in the ballroom, speaking to the king and Ciara's parents. Erica noticed a troubled expression on Brenn's face. Damn, she hoped nothing else was happening. Being robbed in Brenn's home was bad enough.

Laro discreetly got Brenn's attention. Brenn nodded, said something to the king, and walked over to them.

"I hate to disturb you. Erica and I need to speak to you urgently, but we need to find somewhere more private," Laro said.

"Follow me. We can speak in my office." Brenn quickly led

them into his office and shut the door. "What do you need to speak to me about?"

Erica grimaced. Damn, she hated this. "My sword is gone. I believe someone entered my room and stole it. It was in my closet with my other weapons. The scabbard is still there, but the sword is missing."

Brenn cast her a surprised look. "You are sure that is was stolen?"

Erica sighed. "I put it in a safe place. It was in my wardrobe. That's the only explanation I can think of."

"We need to do a thorough search of the estate. Discreetly. I don't want to panic the guests. Find Ivran, Aldis, and Mark. They can assist us and they know their way around. I'll find Ciara. We meet back here in my office."

After leaving Brenn, Erica and Laro found Ivran, Aldis, and Mark. They separated to keep from arousing suspicion and to search the estate efficiently. Erica was dumbfounded. Room after room wasn't disturbed, nothing else missing, and there was no sign of her sword. Frustrated, she went through her head of the list of people that had known about her sword. *Everyone who was at Brenn and Ciara's wedding ceremony.* Her thoughts kept coming back to one person. *Surely it couldn't have been Laura? She was so mesmerized by it. Damn, I hope not.* Laura was the only one she could think of who had taken a lot of interest in her sword but also knew exactly where her room was. If Laura had wanted it, why wouldn't she have taken it earlier?

Finished with her part of the search, she quickly made her way back to Brenn's office. The others had already made it back from their search.

Laro glanced up at her and shook his head. "I couldn't find anything, nor could I find anything else missing."

Everyone except for Mark expressed the same. Nothing

was out of place. Nothing else was missing, except her sword.

Mark looked at her, his jaw clenched. "Several of the crew have left, Laura included. I couldn't find her or the others anywhere."

Erica shook her head. "Laura knew where my room was, and she was fascinated with the sword, but I really can't see her taking it. Are you sure they left? That Laura left? Why would she leave since she's staying here?"

A knock sounded at the door, and Brenn opened it quickly.

Taylith stood there, an unconscious Laura cradled in his arms. Shoving his way inside, he took her to the couch near Brenn's desk and laid her on it. "I found her outside near the flyers. Her scent is off. I think she may have been drugged."

Ciara gasped. Her eyes were glazed, a faraway expression in them. "The king. He is in danger. Taylith, stay with Laura. We have to help the king!"

Erica rushed with the others out of Brenn's office. Erica scanned the room where she knew she had last seen the king. Catching sight of him, she pointed. "There!"

As soon as Erica had spotted him, chaos ensued. The lights flashed off, the many candles doused. The room was pitch black, and screams echoed as people panicked.

Erica tried to continue to where she last saw the king. "I can't see a fucking thing," she said as she stumbled over something on the floor.

Laro grabbed her arm and steadied her. "I can. Stay here, we'll get to him."

"Remain calm, everyone! The lights will be fixed soon," Brenn bellowed.

Erica hated feeling so helpless. She wished she had her pack. At least she would have had some glimmer sticks. Trying hard to see through the inky darkness, she thought she noticed a slight glow. Growls, scuffles, and grunts of pain filled her ears. Suddenly a bright flash of light swooped down. Something clanged loudly against the floor. Chanting overpowered the screams and panicking people's voices. The slight glow grew brighter and brighter, then stopped as the lights flashed back on.

Erica gasped at the scene that lay before her. Icaras held a shield of magic around the king and Cylena. Blood poured from a wound in Biryn's side. Ciara practically glowed with magic, her hands thrown in front of her, a rope of magical flame streaming from her fingers that wound around a sword held mid-flight. A body lay at her feet. Brenn and Laro held two people, knives at their throats. Ivran held another on the floor.

Erica rushed to the scene, her heart sinking as she recognized Brenn and Laro's captives, Gary and Jill. What in the hell were they thinking? She glanced at the one on the floor. It was Ronald. Her crew? Were they responsible for this?

Her heart beat a staccato rhythm — anger, disappointment, frustration, it all attacked her at once.

"Clear everybody out. I will not risk the king further." Brenn growled at the king's guards. "Honored guests, my deepest apologies, but I'm afraid we need to cut this celebration short. The king's guards and my staff will escort you to your flyers and transports."

Erica's sword clattered to the marble tiled floor, blood staining the blade — the king's blood. The discontented members of her crew had put on a fantastic act that evening to seem more at ease with their circumstances, but what in blazes had been the purpose in assassinating the king? What would that serve? Nothing. She bent to pick up the sword, but Brenn stopped her.

"Leave it, Erica. Our investigative team will be here shortly. They will test it for fingerprints."

Though the king had bled profusely, his wound wasn't

145

deep. Ciara healed it, and Biryn scrambled up.

"I am in your debt, Icaras and Ciara. Your fast reaction saved me," Biryn told them, looking at them gratefully.

"Take these three to the dungeons," Brenn ordered several of the king's guards.

Erica felt like crumbling, screaming, crying, as she watched the guards clap her crewmates in irons and lead them away. Why had they used her sword for the assassination? Her thoughts drifted to Laura. "I'm going to see how Laura is," she said and hurried off to Brenn's office, her heart breaking into a million pieces.

CHAPTER FIFTEEN

Taylith sat on his knees beside the couch, his hand on Laura's forehead. Her eyes were open.

"Erica?"

Erica sat on the side of the couch and took Laura's hand in her own. "How are you feeling?"

"Okay now. What happened?"

"That's what we'd like to know. Taylith found you beside a flyer outside in the courtyard, unconscious. It seems you were drugged."

"Really? The last I remember is walking outside with Gary, Jill, and Ronald." She stopped for a moment and frowned. "It's all hazy."

"She needs to rest," Taylith told Erica.

"Wait. I remember something. A green drink. Jill told me it was a special Ierilian alcohol and that it was delicious. It was sweet, like a menthol liqueur."

Laura's words were slurred. Erica switched on her communicator. "Laro, can you get a strong black coffee for Laura from the kitchens?"

"Is she all right?"

"She'll be fine when the drug is out of her system. Coffee, please?"

Laura struggled to sit, but Taylith pushed her back to the couch.

"The sword..." she suddenly said. "Erica's sword."

"What about my sword, Laura?"

"I... I... I'm sssorrry..." Laura burst into tears.

Laro entered with a steaming mug of black coffee. "The king's guards want to question her as soon as she's able to stand."

Taylith protested. "Laura needs to rest. Bed is the best place for her right now."

Laura stopped crying and reached out to touch his face. "You're so sweet," she murmured.

Mm, another romance happening here? "Laura, there was an assassination attempt on the king. Drink the coffee. You have no choice but to answer their questions."

That caused Laura to push Taylith's hand away and sit up straight, a hand to her forehead. "No! You're kidding me, right?"

"Drink the coffee, Laura," Erica prodded gently and held the mug to her lips.

After Laura had consumed half of the coffee, she became calmer and more lucid.

"Erica, please forgive me."

"For what, honey?"

"I told them your sword was magical. They wanted to see and hold it, so I took them to your room. I knew you kept your weapons in your closet. You showed me a while ago."

"And then what happened?"

"I don't know much after that. I began to feel really dizzy. They took me back outside, and that's the last I remember."

"You were found near one of the flyers."

Laura frowned. "Wait, when we were walking in the gardens, Jill mentioned how much Julia missed me and that I should go back with them to the compound."

"She was fed an elixir made from bindweed leaves. It is a forbidden drug on Ierilia, but bindweeds grow in abundance in various places, and people make the drug themselves, then sell it to those addicted to it. As an elixir, it's quite pleasant but causes euphoria, intimate desires, and hallucinations if consumed in great quantities," Taylith told them.

"How do you know?" Erica asked.

"Her description. Green, sweet, menthol tasting, although I am not sure what that word *menthol* means, but it's a pleasant taste. Citizens often consume it for pleasure, but there's a harsh penalty if caught making it or consuming it."

Brenn came in. "How is she? Can she answer questions?"

Laura drank the last of her coffee and struggled to stand. "I'm fine. How is the king?"

"The king is fine. He and his entourage have left for the palace, but several of his imperial guards are still here. They need to question you."

"Brenn, she's told me quite a bit. I think she'll be okay to answer their questions," Erica said.

"They also want to question all of your crew, Erica, except the new arrivals. Are you all right with that?"

"Of course. I'll do anything to cooperate."

Brenn nodded. "Good. Taylith, can you take Laura to the ballroom? They're waiting. I need to speak to Erica alone for a moment."

Laro came to stand beside Erica.

"You, too, Laro. This is private. Close the door," Brenn said.

Laro sent Brenn a strange look but left, closing the door behind him.

"Okay, what's so secretive that only I can hear it?" Erica asked.

"Erica, your sword. My sword. They're very special. There are only four of them in existence. The king has one, and the remaining sword disappeared centuries ago. These swords were forged many centuries ago, before King Tyrol united our planet. They are infused with a magick unlike the other swords forged in Xynnar." Brenn gave her a penetrating look. "What I am about to tell you is highly classified, and I do so only by order of the king. The king cannot be killed. Yes, he can be wounded. But no shot from a fleet weapon, or a thrust from a sword, can actually end his life. The only weapons that can kill him are these swords. Our swords, the king's own sword, though the king seldom carries his. It hangs on his wall as an ornament. When the king presented the sword to you, he honored you greatly by trusting you with his life."

Erica gasped in surprise. "That's a lot to absorb. Will the king be safe at the palace?"

"He will be safe. Aldis is with him."

She paced back and forth. Suddenly she faced him. "How would my crew know that my sword could kill the king? And what would be the purpose of killing him? I know some of my crew are not happy with their circumstances, but killing the king isn't going to help them. There is something more to this."

"My thoughts exactly. Ciara and I think Zohmes is behind this somehow."

"Why would Zohmes attack the king? And use my people to do it?"

Brenn rubbed his chin. "We don't know yet. Did anything unusual happen this evening regarding your crew?"

Erica shook her head. "Not tonight. Nothing that I can think of. During the party, they seemed at ease, almost as if they were in acceptance of remaining on Ierilia."

Brenn lifted an eyebrow. "That is a fast change of heart. Anything else come to mind?"

"Yes, John. Tonight, he was friendly. He asked me questions about Niqine and a book she had been guarding. He'd heard gossip about it. He also didn't quite seem like himself. I mean, he's been rebellious, but I knew John for two years during our training. Right now, he doesn't seem like the same man," Erica said.

"Strange. This conversation is classified. You are now a captain of my legions. As such you are under my command. You cannot divulge our conversation to anyone, not even Laro."

"What's going to happen to my crew members, Brenn?"

"They will be treated like any other criminals. They will stand trial. Attempting to kill the king is a more than serious crime, one punishable by death."

"Oh my God! No, that can't be!" she shouted.

"Erica, I am so sorry, but they will be treated the same as our citizens."

Erica resumed her pacing. He was right. On Earth, they would receive the death penalty, but there would be appeals and more appeals. It could take years before a death sentence was carried out. "I'm sorry, Brenn. They are not above the law. I understand. It's just that, after crashing and surviving, it seems really harsh. I just can't believe my crew going to such measures. Maybe they were drugged, too?"

"I know. Believe me, they'll be questioned, and we'll get to the bottom of it all."

"What am I going to tell Laro?"

"Laro is a commissioned officer now. He will need to understand that sometimes classified information can only be shared with some. If he gives you any problems, tell me, and I'll talk to him."

They left his office and returned to the ballroom. Icaras and Cylena stood looking kind of forlorn near the huge fireplace. Erica walked up to them. "Cylena, I'm sorry your celebration was cut short in such an awful way." She took Cylena's hand and squeezed it.

Cylena smiled. "I am just happy that the king was all right. It could have been a lot worse. He is a very nice man."

And very enamored by you. The girl was so innocent. Girl? She was a young woman. But she'd been so hidden from society, so sheltered, she was still like a girl. She and Icaras both needed to do a lot of growing up. "Yes, he is. Why don't we all retire for the night? I think they've finished questioning Laura. Laro?"

She looked behind her, but Laro was not there. Her heart sank a notch or two. He was insulted that he couldn't be present when Brenn talked to her. How could she tell him there were certain secrets she had to keep, that she couldn't share with him?

Approaching Laura, she noticed her pale face. "Laura? You okay?"

"I am. I'm very upset how my teammates used me," she said softly.

"I know, hon, I understand. Imagine how I feel that it was my sword that wounded the king. Come, I'll take you to your room. You can stand a good night's rest."

"What hurts me the most is that Julia is party to all this."

Erica put an arm around Laura's shoulders and hugged her. "Yes. I'm sorry."

After she tucked Laura in, Erica hastened to her own room and looked at the chaos she'd made when searching for the sword. Shrugging, she merely straightened the quilt and climbed onto the bed without bothering to undress. She was absolutely exhausted. For just a moment, she was disappointed that Laro wasn't with her, but then sleep overtook her.

Two bags of sand were weighing her eyelids down. Erica struggled out of a deep sleep. The twin suns' rays illuminated the room, making the chaos look even worse. The staff would tidy it all up, she knew, but felt guilty. All she wanted and needed right now was a bath, then a coffee.

She'd no sooner had her bath and was toweling her hair when the door opened a crack. "Erica?"

It was Laro.

"Nice of you to show up," she snapped.

"I didn't think you wanted my company last night," he said as he walked in and tried to take her into his arms.

"Get away from me. I needed you last night and where the hell were you?"

"Starshine, so did Tomas. You had enough to deal with last night."

Erica let out a deep breath. Of course, Tomas would have been scared after last night's events. "I just needed your comforting arms around me. I wouldn't have minded Tomas being here, too."

"I'm sorry. There is much we need to learn about each other. What did Brenn tell you? There should be no secrets between us."

"No, there shouldn't be. But this is classified by order of the king. I can't share this information with anyone."

"I may not like secrets between us, but I understand why you can't tell me. Come here," he said and took her into his arms.

She sank against his chest, thankful that he was with her now. "Last night was hell. I can't stop thinking about my crew in the dungeons."

"Finding out that people you trusted are traitors has to be very hard."

"More than that. I don't understand any of it. Poor Cylena, her welcoming celebration shot to hell and back. The girl hasn't been exposed to the world her whole life, and she gets welcomed to society by this? And it's my crew that did it?"

"How is Laura?"

"I took her to her room and put her to bed. Hopefully, she slept the night. Let's go downstairs for breakfast."

Most everyone was in the kitchen eating breakfast when they got there. "Morning, Erica, Laro," several of them greeted.

Erica sat next to Laura. "Honey, how are you?"

"I'm fine, except deeply disturbed about last night."

"I understand that. You and I both," Erica said.

"Erica, your sword is in my office. You can fetch it anytime," Brenn told her.

"Thank you."

Deep down, the sword now scared her. The fact that it had magical qualities was already quite something, but that it was one of the few weapons that could actually kill the king, that was terrifying. She had so many questions, so much playing on her mind. Why the hell couldn't the king be killed? What did she really know about Biryn? He wasn't a shapeshifter lion, or a dragon, nor a sorcerer, so what in the hell was he? The whole evening played on her mind. Her crew and the assassination attempt, her sword... Laro. If she had stayed with her crew and taken charge, none of this would have happened. She pushed her plate away and stood from the table. "I need to get some fresh air." She walked outside to the garden.

Erica stared at the fish swimming in the pond. Her eyes burned with the tears threatening to spill down her face. Everything she touched seemed to turn sour. The loss of her husband and daughter, the crashing of her ship, and the betrayal of her crew. Every time she tried to take a step forward, something important to her was taken away. She couldn't bear it if Laro were taken from her, too.

Arms encircled her from behind and pulled her into a warm embrace. She sank into that warmth, needing the strength, needing him. "Everything I have ever loved has been taken away or turned sour, Laro. How is all of this going to work? How are *we* going to work?"

He kissed the top of her head, holding her tighter in his arms. "We love each other, starshine, and we take each day as the blessing it is."

She turned in his embrace and wrapped her arms around his neck. He tilted her chin up and captured her lips in a kiss that was a promise for a future of love and passion. A future of happiness and joy. "I love you," she whispered against his lips. Laro looked down at her and grinned, flashing that dimple that intrigued her so much. Smiling back at him, it struck her how damn lucky she truly was, and she wasn't about to ever let him go. "Can we tell the others our news?"

He pulled her toward the house. "Come on, they are still at the breakfast table."

They quickly made their way to the kitchen. Laro was right, everyone was still there, choosing the solace of each other's company while waiting for further news about the king.

Ciara looked up as they walked in and smiled widely, a knowing look on her face. "You accepted! We need—"

Erica held her hand up and shook her head, abruptly cutting Ciara off. "Oh, no, no. Don't even think about it. Your parties always seem to end with a bang. I am not going to jinx us."

Laughter went around the room. Ivran and Brenn exchanged knowing glances.

"By party, I am assuming a celebration?" Brenn asked.

"Wait, what did she accept?" Laura asked at the same time.

Laro held up his hand to quiet everyone and pulled Erica against him. "Erica has accepted to be my lifemate. And no, please, no more celebrations." He caught Erica's gaze. "I think we would rather have a small, quiet ceremony in the Clyss."

Erica agreed with him. "Yes, very small and very quiet."

Brenn nodded. "I understand your wishes. Though I hate to break up our small celebration of your news, we have an official meeting with the king. King Biryn wishes to discuss the attempt on his life. Erica, Laro, Icaras, and Ivran, you are to attend as well."

Erica pulled at the collar of her Ierilian dress uniform. It was itchy, and the straps were uncomfortable. She much preferred their battle suits over this one, but Brenn said it was official, so here they were, waiting in front of the king's private rooms, decked out in full regalia, uncomfortable together. She glanced over at Laro. Even with that scowl on his face he was sexy as hell in his uniform.

Footsteps sounded along the foyer, drawing her attention. King Brokig entered the waiting room, Taylith by his side. To Erica's shock, Taylith wore a sword that looked much like her and Brenn's swords. *Is that the missing sword?* The dragons had been under Cewrick's curse for centuries. It made sense that the sword disappeared along with them. She thought better than to ask about it.

King Brokig walked to Ciara. "Good, you are already here. We have much to discuss with King Biryn. Is he doing well after the attempt on his life?"

"The wound was just a surface cut. I healed it. When he left Brenn's estate last night, he seemed well, but his physician is with him now and should be done shortly," Ciara said.

Erica noticed King Brokig scrutinizing them. His gaze rested on Erica, then on the sword she carried.

"Are you sure, daughter, that it is wise to include so many in this meeting?" King Brokig asked, looking at Ciara.

The king's physician opened a door and stepped out. "The king is ready. He will see you now."

Erica could hear the king growl as she entered his quarters with the others. "Aldis, I am fine. You heard my physician. There is no need to be concerned."

156

King Biryn turned his attention to them and gestured to the couches arranged within the room. "Oh good, have a seat. Let's get on with this meeting. It has been an exhausting night."

Erica took a seat by Laro and glanced at the king. He did look exhausted. His face was pale, and dark smudges tainted the skin under his eyes. It was understandable. After the assassination attempt, she hadn't been able to rest well, either.

"King Biryn. I am glad to see you in good health after last night's attempt on your life. Considering the circumstances and the information I am about to share with you, I would suggest you think about who you wish to hear it. I had intended the meeting to be between you, myself, Ciara and her mate, and Taylith," King Brokig said.

"Father!" Ciara exclaimed.

"King Brokig, I have already considered who I wish to be present." King Biryn gestured toward them. "The people you see here, I trust with my life. They will remain."

King Brokig paced the room. "If that is what you wish, then I will get started. As you know, centuries ago our planet was one of great turbulence, each of our many realms at war with another. We were killing ourselves, as well as our planet."

"Yes, yes, my great-grandfather several times removed, King Tyrol, united the planet under one rule. We have been at peace since. This is history, and the information is available to all," King Biryn said impatiently.

"What I am about to share with you is not. We made sure to obliterate all documentation, recordings, and holographs. I suggest you hear me out as I was alive when King Tyrol united Ierilia. I was his general," King Brokig growled.

Erica grasped Laro's hand. Ciara's father looked like he could breathe fire, and his eyes seemed to flash from dragon to human.

Chagrined, King Biryn sighed. "I am sorry for my impatience, King Brokig. Please continue."

King Brokig continued pacing. "The cause of the wars, the hatred between the realms, was the god Zohmes. Ierilia was a gift given to him upon his mating with the goddess of love and joy, Astiana. Their union was meant to temper the beast. Instead, it brought utter chaos. The gods and goddesses crowned Zohmes king of Ierilia and sent him and his mate to the planet as humans. He ruled the planet with a tight fist of hatred and destruction, much to Astiana's dismay. During their union, a son was born, Rithar. The son was gifted with his father's strength but also with his mother's love. At birth, Rithar was blessed with the power to bind Zohmes to Yanata."

Ciara shook her head in confusion. "Why did you not tell us about Zohmes' son before, Father? You knew when we freed you from the curse that we would have to deal with Zohmes."

"The information wouldn't have helped you. Their son is in the realm of dreams. But the tools he created to bind Zohmes are in our possession—the swords." King Brokig looked pointedly at the sword on King Biryn's wall, then at Taylith, Brenn, and Erica. Erica cringed under his scrutiny. "The swords were forged by Brenn's grandfather and infused with power and magic by the gods and goddesses. They also blessed Rithar with the title God of Justice."

King Brokig stopped pacing. "Rithar was your grandfather. After Zohmes increased his path of destruction, his lust for power, his greed, with the help of the gods and goddesses, Rithar banished Zohmes to Yanata by killing him using his sword. He gave up his status as a god to ensure his father would remain banished."

"But the royal line continued, so Rithar must have mated before his assassination," Erica said.

"Yes, Rithar mated with Rekyja, the king's grandmother. She gave birth to Razota, the king's father, and raised him to be a great king."

"King Brokig, please sit. Your striding within my quarters makes me uncomfortable, and I am starting to find your story very hard to believe. There is no written record of this Rithar or Rekyja in my family line. It starts with King Tyrol and most definitely not Zohmes," the king told him heatedly.

King Brokig sat down directly in front of King Biryn. "Rithar *was* Tyrol! We purged the records of the past and rewrote it. Changed timelines, events, and names. Rithar was your grandfather. Zohmes is your great-grandfather. Have you not ever wondered exactly why you could not be killed by any other means but these swords?"

Erica could feel the tension in the room mounting. What a mess. For King Biryn to find out that what he believed of his family had been a fabrication was shocking enough. But to find out that Zohmes was actually his great-grandfather had to be devastating.

"Your Majesty, if you all live such long lives, where is your family now?" Erica asked.

"Ah, there is so much you still need to learn, Captain. When those of us that live for so many years become tired, we choose to travel to the realm of dreams. But my father was assassinated by his general, who had one of the swords. It is that sword that I gifted to Erica. My mother chose to travel to the realm of dreams as she could not live without the man she loved. I was a young man when all this happened. I met Brenn at play in a field when we were very young. We became close friends. Aldis saved my life, or my father's assassin would have killed me, too. I now realize Zohmes must have been involved."

Ciara nodded. "I think Zohmes wanted your father and you both gone so that he would be released from Yanata and could claim the throne. That explains this assassination attempt."

"But how is my crew involved? What would have possessed my teammates to attack the king?"

"I have been wondering that myself. I would like them to be tested for drugs in their system. Today. King Biryn?" Ciara said.

Biryn nodded at Aldis. "Make it so, Aldis. Now."

"There are many possibilities we need to consider. Zohmes' involvement in this assassination attempt. If the Earthlings were fed a potion to do his bidding, they wouldn't know what they were doing, much less remember anything," Ciara pondered.

Erica's heart became a bit lighter. The thought of her teammates standing trial on Ierilian soil terrified her, especially after she'd been witness at the trial by fire.

Biryn stood and walked to the sword on his wall. He took it down, stroked it lovingly, then handed it to Brenn. "Have this taken to my vault. For it to be hanging here is an open invitation. You, Taylith, and Erica, when your swords are not in your scabbard strapped to your back, they need to be secured behind a locked door."

"I have a vault," Brenn said.

"As do I in my castle," Taylith agreed.

"With the assassination attempt and the ease at which Erica's crew members obtained her sword, the sight of them is uncomfortable," Biryn said, rubbing his forehead.

King Brokig stood. "I think this meeting is over. Greetings. May the gods and goddesses be with us all."

"To think that it was my sword that was used is devastating. I feel so utterly betrayed," Erica said and was grateful for Laro's hand covering her own.

"Erica, I will keep your sword safe in my vault," Brenn told her.

Suddenly, King Biryn clasped both hands to his head. He stumbled and fell to the floor. Aldis and Ciara rushed to his side. "Biryn, what's wrong?" Aldis asked.

"My head. I can't think."

Ciara produced her vial of tears from the pocket of her dress and dripped a few drops between the king's lips, but he didn't heal. "I don't know what's wrong with him. Maybe what happened last night has now finally overwhelmed him. Aldis, call his aide to help the king to his bed."

A short while later, Aldis came from the king's room. "He appears to be in a sound sleep now. We should all leave. I will inform you of the results of the blood tests on your crew, Erica. After we have the test results, I will personally question them, but I would like you to be present."

As they left the palace, Erica wondered vaguely how long it would be before she learned the test results. Clutching Laro's hand tightly, she said as they climbed into Brenn's flyer, "Will you come with me when they question my teammates? I need you by my side."

Laro gazed down at her. "Starshine, I will be by your side whenever you need me to be, no matter what the future brings us."

BOOK 4 IN THE CRIMSON REALM CHRONICLES

SWORD OF JUDGEMENT – MARCH 2018

The blade of justice is a double-edged sword…

Betrayed by several members of her crew, Erica now finds herself in a race to beat the clock. A rare poison injected into the king's blood from the blade of her sword, threatens his life.

Erica joins her lifemate, Laro, and the rest of the team, on a mission rife with danger to search for the antidote to save the king. With an angry god bent on destroying the royal line by any means possible, the team doesn't know who to trust or what Zohmes' will do next.

Can Erica find a way to prove the innocence of her crewmembers before the blade of judgement falls?

The blade of justice
is a double-edged sword.

Crimson Realm
Chronicles 4

*Sword of
Judgement*

TARYN
JAMESON

GABRIELLA
BRADLEY

SWORD OF JUDGEMENT

EXCERPT

CHAPTER ONE

Biryn sat up and swung his legs over the side of his bed. Grasping his head with both hands, he tried to stand but felt wobbly. "What is wrong with me?" he muttered.

His personal aide rushed to his side. "Your Majesty, you're not well. Your physician advises rest."

"Get away from me, fool." Biryn managed to stand, pulled his nightshirt off over his head, then looked at Raollin. "Who are you? What do you want? Leave me be. I need to attend to a serious matter."

"Majesty, you can't—"

Ignoring Raollin's babbling and attempts to restrain him, Biryn left his room, marched out of his quarters, and headed to the throne room. It hung somewhere in his mind that he needed to attend a meeting, an important meeting, but he couldn't remember what. He hardly noticed the guards discreetly gazing at the floor as he entered.

"Biryn!"

"Who are you? Why are you here?" Biryn asked the man who had rushed to his side and after quickly removing his cloak, draped it around his shoulders.

"Biryn, it's me, Brenn."

His mind cleared a little. Clapping Brenn on the back, he

said, "Brenn, my friend. You are here to beat me at battle theft. I remember now."

"Your Majesty, I'm not here to play the game. Let me take you back to your quarters." Brenn gently tried to urge Biryn back to the doors.

"Why? Let the game begin. Guards, bring the game!"

"Biryn, you're naked," Brenn told him softly.

"Naked?"

"You're not wearing any clothes."

"Clothes? Oh. Who are those women? Why are there females present for our game?"

"Ciara and Erica. We are here for the hearing, Biryn, but let me take you to your quarters so you can get dressed," Brenn said, managing to guide him toward the doors while holding the cloak in place around him. Taking him by the arm, Brenn was able to take him back to his quarters.

Raollin had already laid out Biryn's clothes and stepped forward to assist him. "General, the physician said the king needs to rest. He is not well."

"That much is obvious. Biryn, how about you rest a while longer? We can postpone the hearing."

Biryn felt completely confused. What was Brenn talking about? What hearing?

Brenn steered him to his bed and waited until he lay down. "We'll talk about it later, after you rest. Try to sleep, Biryn. You'll feel better when you wake."

Biryn saw the woman behind Brenn and tried to sit but something heavy weighed him down. He fought the drowsiness that suddenly attacked him, but it was no use. The dizziness dissipated and he felt himself falling into a deep, dark pit.

BOOK 5 IN THE CRIMSON REALM SERIES:
TESTING THE CROWN – MAY 2018

A throne in peril. The crown challenged…

Born of love and hate, King Biryn must fight between the two. The demons within surface when the woman he loves is abducted by his great-grandfather, the fallen god, Zohmes.

Zohmes wants the throne. His abduction of Cylena ensures that Biryn cannot beget an heir. Imprisoning her in Yanata, the underground world of Ierilia and his to rule, he thinks he is one step further toward the throne and the surface.

Biryn must now face the biggest quest of his life, to defend his throne and crown. He has to travel to Yanata to rescue Cylena. With his team, his family, and the help of the god Izarus, he descends to the heinous bowels of Ierilia.

Will they be able to save his future queen? Can they defeat Zohmes once and for all and bind him forever to Yanata?

BOOK 6 IN THE CRIMSON REALM SERIES:
SHARD IN THE MIRROR – JULY 2018

How does a dragon tell the woman he loves that it was he who had delivered her into the hands of the enemy?

Enslaved as one of Cewrick's feared black dragons, for centuries Taylith had been forced to do the evil sorcerer's bidding. Finally free of the shackles of slavery, Taylith is enlisted by King Biryn as a member of his elite team.

Plagued with visions of an impending war and the return of the black dragon he once was, Taylith must find a way to tell his lifemate, Laura, that he was the creature that had captured her and delivered her into the hands of the enemy.

To keep Laura safe and save her sister from Zohmes' clutches, he must allow the god to change him back into the feared creature he once was.

BOOK 7 IN THE CRIMSON REALM SERIES: INITIATION GENESIS – SEPTEMBER 2018

Starting anew on an alien planet, is no mean task—especially if that planet is rife with magic, shapeshifters, dragons, not to mention a fallen evil god, and a villainous sorcerer.

Now that the king and queen have granted the people from Earth their own realm, Bernie Henderson has been elected to rule it and oversee the building of their new city.

Zohmes and Odoxon have not given up. Bernie finds himself immersed in the trials and tribulations of Ierilia. How will this affect his budding interest in Julia, the mother of Zohmes' son?

Also available in September, **THE LION'S STOWAWAY**, a novella based on the Ierilian world and its characters will be published in an anthology with Viola Grace and other authors. Buy it at extasybooks.com and please help to support the authors by purchasing directly from the publisher!

ABOUT THE AUTHORS

Taryn Jameson is a mother, artist, and avid reader who lives in an enchanted forest that sparks her imagination to create. Her latest outlet is the written word. She is the alter ego of cover artist Angela Waters.

Gabriella Bradley is a mother, a grandmother, and runs a busy business. She has been a writer and artist all her life. Her hobbies include hiking, gardening, swimming, sewing, embroidery. Favorite movies are old timers like Gone with the Wind, Spartacus etc. Favorite TV series ire Fringe and Lost, Favorite music is Abba.

www.ingramcontent.com/pod-product-compliance
Lightning Source LLC
Chambersburg PA
CBHW071249130626
46556CB00003B/1239